~ For Bette Ripke ~
hoping you will
find friends in here,
Naomi Shihab Nye
1996
7-26-96
Keular

p.152

TRANSLATION
TRADUÇÃO
TRADUZIONE
TRADUCCION

PARAGUAY
PILIPINAS
PILIPINAS
REPUBLIK INDONESIA
THAILAND
THAILAND
SVERIGE 5 KR
POST·PAR AVION
SVERIGE 250
ČESKOSLOVENSKO
ČESKOSLOVENSKO
ČESKOSLOVENSKO

THIS SAME SKY

A Collection of Poems from around the World

Selected by NAOMI SHIHAB NYE

ALADDIN PAPERBACKS

A NOTE TO READERS:
At the time this book went to press, several areas around the world were in the midst of political turmoil and upheaval. Because of this poets are sometimes presented with the region rather than the country from which they come.

First Aladdin Paperbacks edition May 1996
Copyright © 1992 by Naomi Shihab Nye
Pages 203–207 constitute an extension of the copyright page.
Aladdin Paperbacks
An imprint of Simon & Schuster
Children's Publishing Division
1230 Avenue of the Americas
New York, NY 10020
Also available in a Simon & Schuster Books for Young Readers edition
Map by Virginia Norey
Designed by Christy Hale
Part-title art by Deborah Maverick Kelley
The text of this book was set in Weiss.
Printed and bound in the United States of America
10 9 8 7 6 5 4 3 2 1

The Library of Congress has cataloged the hardcover edition as follows:
This same day : a collection of poems from around the world
   / selected by Naomi Shihab Nye.—1st ed.
      p. cm.
   Includes bibliographical references and index.
   Summary: A poetry anthology in which 129 poets from sixty-eight different countries celebrate the natural world and its human and animal inhabitants.
   ISBN 0-02-768440-7
   1. Children's poetry. 2. Children's poetry—Translations into English. [1. Poetry—Collections.] I. Nye, Naomi Shihab.
PN6109.97.T49 1992
808.81′936—dc20   92-11617
ISBN 0-689-80630-2 (Aladdin pbk.)

For the wonderful educators I have been privileged to know over the years, especially Harriett B. Lane, John D. Brantley, William O. Walker, Francisco Treto–Garcia, Claude Zetty, Robert Flynn, Carol Mengden, Mary Howard, Paul Rode, Amy Freeman Lee, Maury Maverick, Jr., Bill White, Rubina Schroeder, Sandee Willis, Donna Northouse, Leonard Nathan, William Stafford, Kim Stafford, Rosemary Catacalos, Brenda Goins, Barbara Orlovsky, Christine Eastus, Samuel Hazo, Lorna Hung, and Carolyn Helfman, who encouraged me to gather this book.

CONTENTS

FAMILIES: *"The First Tying"*

THIS EARTH AND SKY IN WHICH WE LIVE:
"Water That Used to Be a Cloud"

INTRODUCTION

The Turkish poet Kandemir Konduk writes about the "apple worm": "All he knows, all he has seen, all his joys, all his cares, are as big as his apple."

We cannot live like the apple worm, as much as we may enjoy thinking about him. From over on the next tree, voices are calling to us—from the next orchard even! How are our branches different and our stories similar? And what lovely, larger life becomes ours when we listen to one another?

Poetry has always devoted itself to bringing us into clearer focus—letting us feel or imagine faraway worlds from the inside. During the Gulf War of 1991, when the language of headline news seemed determined to push human experience into the "sanitized" distance, I found myself searching for poems by Iraqi poets to carry into classrooms. Even if the poems had been written decades earlier, they helped to give a sense of human struggle and real people living behind those headlines.

Those of us living in the United States often suffer from a particular literary provinciality, imagining ourselves to be the primary readers and writers of the planet. We forget that our literary history is relatively brief. Writers in Bangalore, India, asked me what it is like to live in a country with "such a young soul." When a writer in Dhaka, Bangladesh, said, "We try so hard to know what people are writing in the United States—do people in your country try as hard to know about us?" I felt ashamed.

Over the years, working as a poet-in-the-schools, I have taken special pleasure in finding poems from many countries that are accessible to younger readers. Not only may we discover more about writing through these poems, but we may also catch a glimpse of so many distant friends. I think of a house with a thousand glittering windows. I think of poets over the ages sending their voices out into the sky, leaving quiet, indelible trails.

A. Z. M. Obaidullah Khan of Bangladesh has written, "Every true word uttered by the tongue/is poetry/Every ear of corn in the ploughed land/is poetry/One who has no ear for poetry/Shall hear only the moaning of the storm/One who has no ear for poetry/Shall lose the inheritance of the horizons . . ."

Because of the number of fine anthologies featuring poets from the United States that have appeared in recent years, I have decided not to include writers who were born in the United States in this book. The poets here have shared the twentieth century from many other vantage points.

Deep appreciation to the dedicated translators who labored on all horizons to make these border-crossings possible. Whenever someone suggests "how much is lost in translation!" I want to say, "Perhaps—but how much is gained!" A new world of readers, for one thing.

This book gathers long-favorite poems together with others that were sent directly to be considered for this volume. The poets of Guyana, South America, and Mauritius, Indian Ocean, were particularly generous with their correspondences. Special gratitude to Don Hausrath of the United States Information Agency for spreading the word about this anthology, to Arthur Sze in New Mexico, and to Frank Stewart of *Manoa* journal, who shared his wonderful contacts in the Philippines.

I am particularly grateful, as well, to editor Virginia Duncan of Four Winds Press for her energy, belief, and sensitive care, and to Soyung Pak and Andrea Schneeman for all they did to get this book flying.

Together, from our apples, we grow.

Naomi Shihab Nye
San Antonio, Texas
1992

HOUSE OF SPRING

Hundreds of open flowers
    all come from
        the one branch
Look
    all their colors
        appear in my garden
I open the clattering gate
    and in the wind
        I see
the spring sunlight
    already it has reached
        worlds without number

Musō Soseki
Japan
Translated by W. S. Merwin
and Soiku Shigematsu

WORDS AND SILENCES

"Sawdust from under the Saw"

Once I got a postcard from the Fiji Islands
with a picture of sugar cane harvest. Then I realized
that nothing at all is exotic in itself.
There is no difference between digging potatoes in
     our Mutiku garden
and sugar cane harvesting in Viti Levu.
Everything that is is very ordinary
or, rather, neither ordinary nor strange.
Far-off lands and foreign peoples are a dream,
a dreaming with open eyes
somebody does not wake from.
It's the same with poetry—seen from afar
it's something special, mysterious, festive.
No, poetry is even less
special than a sugar cane plantation or potato field.
Poetry is like sawdust coming from under the saw
or soft yellowish shavings from a plane.
Poetry is washing hands in the evening
or a clean handkerchief that my late aunt
never forgot to put in my pocket.

Jaan Kaplinski
Estonia
Translated by the poet, Riina Tamm, and Sam Hamill

OLD MOUNTAINS WANT TO TURN TO SAND

I have my roots inside me,
a skein of red threads.
The stones have their roots inside them,
like fine little ferns.

Wrapped around their softness
the stones sleep hard.
For centuries they have rested
under the sun.

Old mountains
want to turn to sand.
They let themselves go
and open up to water.

After centuries of thirst!
Like language—
that great mountain broken up
by our tongues.

We turn language to sand,
immersing the tongue
in a running stream
that moves mountains.

Tommy Olofsson
Sweden
Translated by Jean Pearson

THE MEANING OF SIMPLICITY

I hide behind simple things so you'll find me;
if you don't find me, you'll find the things,
you'll touch what my hand has touched,
our hand-prints will merge.

The August moon glitters in the kitchen
like a tin-plated pot (it gets that way
    because of what I'm saying to you),
it lights up the empty house and
    the house's kneeling silence—
always the silence remains kneeling.

Every word is a doorway
to a meeting, one often cancelled,
and that's when a word is true:
    when it insists on the meeting.

Yannis Ritsos
Greece
Translated by Edmund Keeley

POETRY WAS LIKE THIS

Poetry was the memory of adolescence.
It was my mother's sad face,
the yellow bird on a *neem* tree,
my little brothers and sisters
    sitting at night around a fire
    of dry fallen leaves,
father's home-coming,
the ringing of a bicycle bell—*Rabeya, Rabeya*—
and the opening of the southern door
at the sound of my mother's name.

Poetry was wading through a knee-deep river
across a fog-laden path,
the morning call for prayer, or the burning of paddy stalks
after the harvesting, the lovely dark dots of rye
on the plump crust of a homemade country cake,
the smell of fish, a fishing-net spread out
on the courtyard to dry,
and Grandpa's grave under a cluster of bamboo leaves.

Poetry was an unhappy boy growing up in the forties,
a truant pupil's furtive attendance at public meetings,
freedom, processions, banners, the piteous story
of a fierce communal riot told by my elder brother,
    returning from the holocaust a pauper.

Poetry was a flock of birds on a *char* land,
carefully collected bird's eggs,
fragrant grass, the runaway calf of a sad-looking
         young farm wife,
neat letters on secret writing pads in blue envelopes.
Poetry was Ayesha Akhter of my village school
    with her long loose flowing hair.

Al Mahmud
Bangladesh
Translated by Kabir Chowdhury

Notes: *Neem* is the Bengali word for the margosa tree. The wind blowing through the
leaves of this big tree is believed to be capable of healing the sick.

The sandy strips of land rising out of the beds of rivers are known as *char* in Bengali.

THE PEN

Take a pen in your uncertain fingers.
Trust, and be assured
That the whole world is a sky-blue butterfly
And words are the nets to capture it.

Muhammad al-Ghuzzi
Tunisia
Translated by May Jayyusi and John Heath-Stubbs

THE QUESTION MARK

Poor thing. Poor crippled measure
of punctuation. Who would know,
who could imagine you used to be
an exclamation point?
What force bent you over?
Age, time and the vices
of this century?
Did you not once evoke,
call out and stress?
But you got weary of it all,
got wise, and turned like this.

Gevorg Emin
Armenia
Translated by Diana Der Hovanessian

THE GATHERER

Blooming gardens are my words
My words are dusky gardens . . .
Gather them O bamboo pen . . .
And drink to inebriation from an ink pot . . .
My words are like flowers . . .
Exuding fragrance,
When pressed by the scorching summer . . .
Gather them O bamboo pen.
For tonight I want to write about Sid Ahmed —
A milkman was he.
The milk drowned in water.
O Sid Ahmed!
And we are liars . . .
I, the chief of the quarter and the mayor.
Gather my words O bamboo pen,
For I intend to talk about a silk cap
Glowing on a bridegroom's head . . .
And about Aisha the Taamia vendor
And about Gebran the Yemeni
And about a bean pot on a dry wood fire
And about the kids in the local school —
Chanting "ja, ha, kha, la, ka, wa'l"
. . . let us remember Musa, the chatterbox,

And Ibrahim the tattletale,
And Eissa, dry as wood,
And do not forget laughing Ishaq.
And our teacher Sheikh Al-Bushra . . .
Sheikh Al-Bushra was . . . .
Silence!!
Honor the teacher . . .   . . .

Ali al-Mak
The Sudan
Translated by al-Fatih Mahjoub and Constance E. Berkley

LIZARD

The beginning of a lizard
almost always becomes: Lizard.

The lizard rather easily reaches
the result: Lizard.

The beginning of a lizard
almost never becomes a sparrow.

In this way most beings become
their own sort of lizards from the beginning.

Once when I was a human being
quick as lightning I saw a lizard.

Bundgård Povlsen
Denmark
Translated by Poul Borum

BETWEEN EBB AND FLOW

When words grow jellylike
on people's lying lips
I shrink into myself,
I dwindle and recede
avoiding the jellylike trails
    on the roads
and all of human sliminess.
Terrified, I retreat
from the wolf's glamorous smile,
holding myself tightly in
lest I slip,
digging my heels deep
into slippery ground,
closing my hands,
refusing to feel
false smiles
or the gleam of the fox.

But when a little child embraces me
touching my tired face
with a velveteen cheek,
soft hands, lily fingers
lacking claws,
when two lovely eyes
washed by dawn
and the angels of light
gaze into my life,
my heart softens,
my heart grows large,

walls recede
till the melting rivers
of the north pour into it
and the human face
returns from its exile
to dwell inside me.

Fadwa Tuqan
Palestine
Translated by Salma Khadra Jayyusi
and Naomi Shihab Nye

CROWNED CRANE

(1)
Crowned crane
Beautiful crowned crane of power
Bird of the word
Your voice took part in creation;
You the drum and the stick that beats it
What you speak is spoken clearly
Ancestor of praise-singers, even the tree
Upon which you perch is worthy of commendation
Speaking of birds, you make the list complete
Some have big heads and small beaks
Others have big beaks and small heads
But you have self-knowledge;
It is the Creator himself who has adorned you!

(2)
People of this place,
Look, the crowned crane is dancing!
Crowned crane, praise-singing woman
During the day the shameless one weaves,
Astonishing!

(3)
The beginning of beginning rhythm
Is speech of the crowned crane;
The crowned crane says, "I speak."
The word is beauty.

Bamana—traditional folk poem
Mali
English version by Judith Gleason

Note: According to Bamana tribal myth, the crowned crane taught human beings to speak.
This bird has a trumpetlike voice that can cry in two different keys.

A TREE WITHIN

A tree grew inside my head.
A tree grew in.
Its roots are veins,
its branches nerves,
thoughts its tangled foliage.
Your glance sets it on fire,
and its fruits of shade
are blood oranges
and pomegranates of flame.
              Day breaks
in the body's night.
There, within, inside my head,
the tree speaks.
             Come closer—can you hear it?

Octavio Paz
Mexico
Translated by Eliot Weinberger

A SHORT STORY

The ant climbs up a trunk
carrying a petal on its back;
and if you look closely
that petal is as big as a house
especially compared to the ant that
carries it so olympically.

You ask me: Why couldn't I carry
a petal twice as big as my body and my head?

Ah, but you can, little girl,
but not petals from a dahlia,
rather boxes full of thoughts
and loads of magic hours, and
a wagon of clear dreams, and
a big castle with its fairies:
all the petals that form the soul of
a little girl who speaks and speaks . . . !

David Escobar Galindo
El Salvador
Translated by Jorge D. Piche

LIFE OF THE CRICKET

An invalid since time began,
he goes on little green crutches
stitching the countryside.

Incessantly from five o'clock
the stars stream through
his pizzicato voice.

Hard worker, his antennae,
dragging like fish-lines,
troll the high floods of air.

At night a cynic,
he lies inert in his grass house,
songs folded and hung up.

Furled like a leaf,
his folio preserves
the records of the world.

Jorge Carrera Andrade
Ecuador
Translated by John Malcolm Brinnin

COILS THE ROBOT

Coils the robot
named by some scientists
is the smallest one in school.
They sent him to learn
to cope with numbers,
letters and things
but Coils the robot
only understands poetry.
His square tiny tummy
glows in the sun
and rings like a bell
when he dances and sings.
He enlightens his eyes,
his hands are of wire,
his little antenna twinkles magically.
Coils needs love,
oily light, silvery
with the sparkles of sunlight;
deep down inside
his little heart glitters and throbs.

Floria Herrero Pinto
Costa Rica
Translated by Barbara Chacón

FROM *ALTAZOR*

At the horislope of the mountizon
The violinswallow with a cellotail
Slipped down this morning from a lunawing
And hurries near
Look here swoops the swooping swallow
Here swoops the whooping wallow
Here swoops the weeping wellow
Look here swoops the sweeping shrillow
Swoops the swamping shallow
Swoops the sheeping woolow
Swoops the slooping swellow
Look here swoops the sloping spillow
The scooping spellow
The souping smellow
The seeping swillow
The sleeping shellow
Look here swoops the swooping day
And the night retracts its claws like a leopard
Swoops the swapping swallow
With a nest in each of the torrid zones
As I have them on the four horizons
Swoops the snooping smallow
And waves rise on tiptoe
Swoops the whelping whirllow
And the mountain's head feels dizzy

Vicente Huidobro
Chile
Translated by Eliot Weinberger

PAPER DOLL

Paper doll got tired
but said nothing;
she went on letting herself
be written on,
got flooded with ink
and just in time was saved
from dying of the last period
because she climbed onto
a paper ship
and disembarked on the sea.
There, paper doll
started swimming,
and the ocean all around
was, for an instant,
a blue soup of tiny letters.

Guadalupe Morfín
Mexico
Translated by Rául Aceves and Cristina Carrasco
with Jane Taylor

DISTANCES OF LONGING

When you go away and I can't
follow you up with a letter,
it is because the distance
between you and me
    is shorter than the sound of Oh,
because the words are smaller
than the distance
    of my longing.

Fawziyya Abu Khalid
Saudi Arabia
Translated by May Jayyusi

AT THE BEACH

The waves are erasing the footprints
Of those who are walking the beach.

The wind is carrying away the words
Two people are saying to each other.

But still they are walking the beach
Their feet making new footprints.

Still the two are talking together
Finding new words.

Kemal Ozer
Turkey
Translated by O. Yalim, W. Fielder, and Dionis Riggs

MONKEYS

The fact that we
don't understand
their language
doesn't mean
that they don't converse

If they could
understand us
they would
consider us to be
completely incomprehensible
and mad to boot

Klara Koettner-Benigni
Austria
Translated by Herbert Kuhner

FREEDOM

Words, one by one
arrive on the empty page
like honored guests.
Ordered thoughts move
gracefully.
Outside the window,
on the sill,
I see the figure of a bird,
sun on its feathers—
a brownish, medium-sized bird.
I try to wave it away,
but it intrudes more stubbornly.
It has a quizzical look in its eye.
Ignoring its rude presence
I try to compose my lines,
but I feel uneasy
being observed by a brownish, medium-sized bird
with sun on its feathers—

Wimal Dissanayake
Sri Lanka

LAMENTO

He put down his pen.
It lies inert on the table.
It lies inert in space.
He put down his pen.

Too much that can neither be revealed nor concealed!
He's blocked by what's happening elsewhere, apart,
although the magic satchel is throbbing like a heart.

Outdoors it is early summer.
From the greenwood come whistles—of humans or birds?

And cherry boughs in blossom tap the tops of trucks that have come
home.

Weeks go by.
Night slowly comes.
Moths settle on the windowpane:
small pale telegrams from the world.

Tomas Tranströmer
Sweden
Translated by May Swenson with Leif Sjöberg

WORDLESS DAY

There is a wordless tomorrow
In which I'll forget all the chatter
It will be like the sky clearing after a rainstorm
To the washed gray of morning
The distant mountains an ink-black line
Sweeping the mists away from here

But today
Is still a day for cymbals
Percussionists join in the celebration
Raising a din, pounding without restraint

Until twilight when I am so weary
That I long for the sleep
My tongue enjoys inside my mouth

Chang Shiang-hua
Taiwan
Translated by Stephen L. Smith with
Naomi Shihab Nye

DREAMS AND DREAMERS

"Eyes the Color of Sky"

IN THE KITCHEN

The fire crackles in the kitchen range, and big disheveled clouds of steam stick their faces up against the window-panes.

At the table, the child is writing. Leaning over him, the father guides his wobbling hand. "Try!" he says. "That's better—that's good." Then, "It's late."

The child writes, *Child*, and is amazed at this word there on the page, like a friendly animal that soon, when the ink has dried, he'll be able to stroke with his finger.

In his best copperplate hand, the father writes *mirror*, the curves and uprights elegantly curlicued between the lines (he's a copying-clerk at the factory).

Mirror, the child copies; then sighs, "I'm so sleepy." "It's snowing," the father says.

The child writes, "It's snowing," and, in his black red-bordered pinafore, falls peacefully asleep.

Jean Joubert
France
Translated by Denise Levertov

A HEADSTRONG BOY

I guess my mother spoiled me—
I'm a headstrong boy. I want every instant
to be lovely as crayons.

I'd like to draw—on chaste white paper—
a clumsy freedom, eyes that never wept,
a piece of sky, a feather, a leaf,
a pale green evening, and an apple.

I'd like to draw dawn, the smile dew sees,
the earliest, tenderest love—an imaginary love
who's never seen a mournful cloud,
whose eyes the color of sky will gaze at me
forever, and never turn away.
I'd like to draw distance, a bright horizon,
carefree, rippling rivers, hills sheathed in green furze.
I want the lovers to stand together in silence,
I want each breathless moment to beget a flower.

I want to draw a future I've never seen—
nor ever can—though I'm sure she'll be beautiful.
I'll draw her an autumn coat the color of candle flame,
and maple leaves, and all the hearts that ever loved her.
I'll draw her a wedding, an early morning garden party,
swathed in candy-wrappers decked with winter scenes.

I'm a headstrong boy. I want to paint out every sorrow,
to cover the world with colored windows,
let all the eyes accustomed to darkness
be accustomed to light. I want to draw wind,
mountains, each one bigger than the last.
I want to draw the dream of the East,
a fathomless sea, a joyful voice.

Finally, I'd like to draw myself in one corner—
a panda, huddled in a dark Victorian forest,
hunkering in the quiet branches, homeless, lost,
not even a heart left behind me, far away,
only teeming dreams of berries
and great, wide eyes.

This pining's pointless.
I haven't any crayons,
any breathless moments.
All I have are fingers and pain.

I think I'll tear the paper to bits
and let them drift away,
hunting for butterflies.

Gu Cheng
China
Translated by Donald Finkel

WANTING TO MOVE

Continually, a bell rings in my heart.
I was supposed to go somewhere, to some other place,
Tense from the long wait—
Where do you go, will you take me
"With you, on your horses, down the river, with the flame
of your torches?"

They burst out laughing.
"A tree wanting to move from place to place!"
Startled, I look at myself—
A tree, wanting to move from place to place, a tree
Wanting to move? Am I then—
Born here, to die here
Even die here?
Who rings the bell, then, inside my heart?
Who tells me to go, inside my heart?
Who agitates me, continually, inside my heart?

Vijaya Mukhopadhyay
India
Translated by the poet

THE CUCUMBER

To Ekber Babayev

The snow is knee-deep in the courtyard
and still coming down hard:
it hasn't let up all morning.
We're in the kitchen.
On the table, on the oilcloth, spring—
on the table there's a very tender young cucumber,
    pebbly and fresh as a daisy.
We're sitting around the table staring at it.
It softly lights up our faces
and the very air smells fresh.
We're sitting around the table staring at it,
amazed
    thoughtful
        optimistic.
As if we're in a dream . . .
on the table, on the oilcloth, hope—
on the table, beautiful days,
a cloud seeded with a green sun,
an emerald crowd impatient and on its way,
loves blooming openly—
on the table, there on the oilcloth, a very tender young
        cucumber,
    pebbly and fresh as a daisy.
The snow is knee-deep in the courtyard
and coming down hard.
It hasn't let up all morning.

(March 1960, Moscow)
Nazim Hikmet
Turkey
Translated by Randy Blasing and Mutlu Konuk

THE TIN BIRD

There is an amazing bird:
its beak an old umbrella
its body nothing but empty tins
of corned beef and sardines.

It sees with the eyes
of a doll now broken and forgotten.
Its nest is a dump all smelly and rotten.

When the moon rises like a cradle in the sky,
the bird flies and sings and cries:

Sleepytimes, little sleepy heads
of those who have no food.
I am the angel of your dreams.
I am the birdsong of your sighs.

Ugly as I am,
all rusted and torn,
my song is sweet,
my friendship even sweeter.

Sleepytime, sleepytime, o beloved children.
I watch over babies who know no pillows,
over the little sleepyheads who have no suppers.

Ramón C. Sunico
Philippines
Translated by the poet

ON MY BIRTHDAY

On the 9th of August I'll transform
the entire city into an enormous
    birthday cake.
And if the Central Military Office,
the President's House, the banks,
the stadium, the Embassies,
    and the university
raise their heads breaking
    the smooth symmetry
I'll scatter fragrant pistachio nuts
    over them all
so my guests
    will not be disappointed.

Farhad Mazhar
Bangladesh
Translated by Kabir Chowdhury and Naomi Shihab Nye

THE ORPHAN

Oh, the dream! The dream!
My strong, gilded wagon
has collapsed,
its wheels have scattered like gypsies.
One night I dreamt of spring
and when I awoke
flowers covered my pillow.
I dreamt once of the sea.
In the morning my bed was rich
with shells and fins.
But when I dreamt of freedom
spears surrounded my neck
with morning's halo.

From now on you will not find me
at ports or among trains
but in public libraries
sleeping head down on the maps of the world
as the orphan sleeps on pavement
where my lips will touch more than one river
and my tears stream from continent
to continent.

Muhammad al-Maghut
Syria
Translated by May Jayyusi and Naomi Shihab Nye

WILDPEACE

Not that of a cease-fire,
let alone the vision of the wolf and the lamb,
but rather
as in the heart after a great excitement: you can only
talk about the weariness.
I know that I know how
to kill: that's why I'm an adult.
And my son plays with a toy gun that knows
how to open and close its eyes and say Mama.
A peace
without the big noise of beating swords into ploughshares,
without words, without
the heavy thud of the rubber stamp: I want it
gentle over us, like lazy white foam.
A little rest for the wounds—
who speaks of healing?
(And the orphans' outcry is passed from one generation
to the next, as in a relay race:
the baton never falls.)

I want it to come like wildflowers,
suddenly, because the field
needs it: *wildpeace.*

Yehuda Amichai
Israel
Translated by Chana Bloch

HEALING

The nights passed very darkly.
Great cries ran in the wind.
The next day we didn't remember a thing.
There was a deep hole left in time.

There where the wolf had nestled in,
a pothole remained, spread with warm wolf-hair.
Now a sheep could lie down there.

Yannis Ritsos
Greece
Translated by Edmund Keeley

HAPPY AS A DOG'S TAIL

Happy as something unimportant
and free as a thing unimportant.
As something no one prizes
and which does not prize itself.
As something mocked by all
which mocks at their mockery.
As laughter without serious reason.
As a yell able to outyell itself.
Happy as no matter what,
as any no matter what.

Happy
as a dog's tail.

Anna Swir
Poland
Translated by Czesław Miłosz and Leonard Nathan

PICNIC TO THE EARTH

here let's jump rope together   here
here let's eat balls of rice together
here let me love you
your eyes reflect the blueness of sky
your back will be stained a wormwood green
here let's learn the constellations together

from here let's dream of every distant thing
here let's gather low-tide shells,
from the sea of sky at dawn
let's bring back little starfish
at breakfast we will toss them out
let the night be drawn away
here I'll keep saying, "I am back"
while you repeat, "Welcome home"
here let's come again and again
here let's drink hot tea
here let's sit together for awhile
let's be blown by the cooling breeze

Shuntarō Tanikawa
Japan
Translated by Harold Wright

WHY THERE ARE NO CATS IN THE FOREST

A parrot was what
he once had on his left shoulder,
the thought of it,
which came long before
the actual bird
which never came.
It never came.

It was never the season
for parrots
which were unreachable,
which nested on the highest
and deadest of branches
of the tallest tree
in the farthest forest
and he lived in the city
and no one ever promised him a bird
or spoke to him.

And the reason he was now carrying
a stray cat
on the same shoulder
was that the thought of the parrot
would not fly away.

A dream never flies away
but it can be destroyed
or eaten.

Simeon Dumdum, Jr.
Philippines

SONG

I placed my dream in a boat
and the boat into the sea;
then I ripped the sea with my hands
so that my dream would sink.

My hands are still wet
with the blue of the slashed waves,
and the color that runs from my fingers
colors the deserted sands.

The wind arrives from far away,
night bends itself with the cold;
under the water in a boat
my dream is dying away.

I'll cry as much as necessary
to make the sea grow
so that my boat will sink to the bottom
and my dream disappear.

Then everything will be perfect:
the beach smooth, the waters orderly,
my eyes dry like stones
and my two hands—broken.

Cecilia Meireles
Brazil
Translated by Eloah F. Giacomelli

THE SICK-ROOM

When I was frightened by the spots upon the wall
I called them spiders and they moved and ran
Until my parents came to me.
I could not tell the daylight dreams
From dreams when all is dark.
This was the room where all my fears began.

The doctor came, and he was Doctor Gloom
For he was dressed in black. He put the spoon
Into my mouth until it touched my throat
And I was almost sick. He did not know
The bed became my grave and sheets became my earth
And this was loneliness like days upon the moon.

R. A. Simpson
Australia

THE SHADOW INSIDE ME

Night has driven the shadow
into my own body. It's an inward
robe that stretches its arms

and legs into my limbs, whispers
like silk along my spine,
turns darker and darker until it

finally comes off in me as the color
of sleep, behind whose eyelids
two black flames are flickering.

Tommy Olofsson
Sweden
Translated by Jean Pearson

One day I asked the mirror facing me,
Friend, what's true?

> White teeth
> Gray hair
> Black eyes.

Even if it hurts, what else?

> Size 20.

But tell me more.
Am I really beautiful?

> You are indifferent, why?

How about my heart, mirror?
Is it white? Gray?
Is it pure or dirty

> Silence.

O mirror, I see.

I need a human friend
True enough
To reflect my heart.

Tialuga Sunia Seloti
American Samoa

THE PRISON CELL

It is possible . . .
It is possible at least sometimes . . .
It is possible especially now
To ride a horse
Inside a prison cell
And run away . . .

It is possible for prison walls
To disappear,
For the cell to become a distant land
Without frontiers:

—What did you do with the walls?
—I gave them back to the rocks.
—And what did you do with the ceiling?
—I turned it into a saddle.
—And your chain?
—I turned it into a pencil.

The prison guard got angry.
He put an end to the dialogue.
He said he didn't care for poetry,
And bolted the door of my cell.

He came back to see me
In the morning;
He shouted at me:

—Where did all this water come from?
—I brought it from the Nile.
—And the trees?
—From the orchards of Damascus.
—And the music?
—From my heartbeat.

The prison guard got mad;
He put an end to my dialogue.
He said he didn't like my poetry,
And bolted the door of my cell.

But he returned in the evening:

—Where did this moon come from?
—From the nights of Baghdad.
—And the wine?
—From the vineyards of Algiers.
—And this freedom?
—From the chain you tied me with last night.

The prison guard grew so sad . . .
He begged me to give him back
His freedom.

Mahmud Darwish
Palestine
Translated by Ben Bennani

A SAILOR'S MEMOIRS
(excerpts from the twentieth memoir)

I don't believe in a sun
That illuminates caves
While my home remains steeped
In total darkness.
I don't believe in a land
Where thorns and cares
Are my share of its yield
While the harvest belongs to others.
Peace be to the Gulf breeze
Though others claim its pearls.
Peace to the sand of the shores,
Bed of dying dawn.
Peace to past memories that loom
Like a covey of pigeons crossing the sky.
Peace to returning ships
And their singers in moonlight.
Peace to the sails in the Gulf,
Roaming the seas, loving risk.
Peace to him who goes out pearl-diving,
And to him who returns from a voyage.
Peace be to women beating tambourines
And their triumphant vows that make dreams
Come true.
Peace be to a gathering in the dark
Lit up by songs and vibrant strings.

Peace to him who winds cables,
To our neighborhoods in winter,
Their paths awash with rain.
Peace be to the neighborhood water-carrier,
His jingling bells in the passageways.
Peace to the well in the morning,
Its sputtering bucket as it descends.
Peace to the brazier in winter
Around which are spun the evening tales.
Peace be to the rampart and its turrets,
The stones and boards of its gates.
Peace be to our quiet dwellings,
As still as the dead in their tombs.
They almost push away the huge buildings
To tell their own past stories.
I almost smell lost generations in them,
Lying underneath us without veils.
They peep at me through the wall cracks
And complain of insomnia.
Peace! Peace! For I am gone
Like gathered clouds that pour down
To be drunk by hard rocks,
To fill skin-bags and streams.

Muhammad al-Fayiz
Kuwait
Translated by Issa Boullata and Naomi Shihab Nye

Where is the heart I am calling?
Heart become eyelid
of an eye on its way to where I am.
The eye is not here yet and already I can see.
Before there is a heart I am made of beating.
I am calling in an open doorway.
I am calling from inside.

Roberto Juarroz
Argentina
Translated by W. S. Merwin

DAY-DREAM

There is nobody anywhere near him.
The boy unwinds his kite string by himself.
The shapely piece of paper called him out
early in the morning. He came into the sky.
Space is calligraphic in the clouds. The boy
understands although no one else may read it.
The kite does not want to return to earth
and keeps watch for a possible second kite.
The society of the blue will be shaken and
birds take fright when the two painted squares
attack each other, embrace and weep until one
drops, falling face down in the boy's daydream.

Samarendra Sengupta
India
Translated by Lila Ray

THE PARAKEETS

They talk all day
and when it starts to get dark
they lower their voices
to converse with their own shadows
and with the silence.

They are like everybody,
the parakeets:
all day chatter
and at night bad dreams.

With their gold rings
on their clever faces,
brilliant feathers
and the heart restless
with speech.

They are like everybody,
the parakeets:
the ones that talk best
have separate cages.

Alberto Blanco
Mexico
Translated by W. S. Merwin

A DREAM OF PARADISE IN THE SHADOW OF WAR

Sometimes
In the tangled boughs
Of the jasmine tree
And sometimes
On the green emerald floor
A nightingale sings
The poignant melodies
Of love.
From the vast treeless plains
Carried by the evening's dust-clouds
Come the joyous sounds
Of people returning home.
Mustard fields stretch
Towards the horizon.
Wild roses and green swaying wheat.
The cacophony of birds
On the ancestral tree
In my courtyard.
The houses and their inmates
Stand amazed.
The village-wilderness
Turns into a perfumed garden.

Muneer Niazi
Pakistan
Translated by Daud Kamal

SALT AND MEMORY
A tribute to Marc Chagall

When you arrive in our town
I would like to sit on the roof
and play the violin, play the violin,
play—it is good that you live
sweet old man sweet sweet
sweet even as was my father
your sixty-six thousand colors glitter
on the walls of my sixty-six years
bearded sky bearded dawn
bearded smoke of my childhood
your candles burn in my window on
hills that grew from bones of the dead
bundle-carrying shadows carry
salt and memories in their headband
thc calf steps out of the cow's belly
so it can lick your hand

Zoltán Zelk
Hungary
Translated by Barbara Howes

MY GREAT GRAND UNCLE

My great grand uncle had a peculiar hobby.
He used to collect the feathers
    of different kinds of birds
    of different colours, from different places.
His bedroom, corridor and staircase
Were full of thousands of colourful, colourless feathers.

On the day of his death
Just before sunrise, at dawn,
My great grand uncle
    went to the rooftop of his house
And threw the feathers into the morning air.
The feathers floated in the golden rays
        of the rising sun.
Some of the feathers dropped near.
Some went far.
Some floated towards eternity, the sky.

No, it is not possible to write a story
        on this subject
But some feathers are still floating
        in the sky.

Tarapada Ray
India
Translated by the poet

MAGIC

Today I'm a hill,
tomorrow a sea.
Always wandering
like Miriam's well,
always a bubble
lost in the gorges.

Last night I dreamt
red horses, purple,
green—

In the morning I listened:
an endless babbling of water,
a chatter of parrots.

Today I'm a snail,
tomorrow a giant
palm tree.

Yesterday a cave,
today I'm a seashell.
Tomorrow
I'll be tomorrow.

Dahlia Ravikovitch
Israel
Translated by Chana Bloch and
Ariel Bloch

FAMILIES

"The First Tying"

WOLF-ANCESTRY

Under the linden in Sands
My great grandfather
Found two wolf-cubs

Sat them both
Between a donkey's ears
And brought them to the farm

He fed them sheep's milk
And taught them to play
With lambs their own age

Then he took them back
to the same spot under the lindens
Kissed them
And made the sign of the cross over them

Since earliest childhood
I've been waiting
For my years to equal
My great grandfather's

Just to ask him
Which of those wolf-cubs
I was

Vasko Popa
Yugoslavia
Translated by Charles Simic

TO THE ANCESTORS

Clearers of thornbush,
>   Receive our morning greetings,
You who graded clefts in the cliffs,
>   Receive our morning greetings,
You who laid the cornerstone,
>   Receive our morning greetings,
You who placed the three hearthstones,
>   Receive our morning greetings,
And you, women, who carried long-stemmed calabashes,
>   Receive our morning greetings.

Dogon—traditional folk poem
Mali
English version by Judith Gleason

Note: Calabashes are gourds that are used for carrying liquids, serving foods, and storing items.

CHILDHOOD

Evening. Grandmother scolding the white chickens—
and that red one a fox would leave lying in its own
blood one night.

They came running through the yard, illuminated,
seen through a leaded window's immense pane of
mauve, in a haze of flies, vesper-bells, the tiny birds
called tomtits.

Everything dancing, westering sun, hail of grain
hitting the old tin plate's violet enamel veined with
cracks, and bits of straw spinning in a puddle.

Among the dahlias by the pump, the hunchbacked
tree crosses itself.

The forest's black ink pours in around us: storm,
dense, shadow of wild boar.

So much beauty, so much fear! Was I crying? That
poor hand led me through the garden.

The house was steaming itself in a dream of laundry.
I want to tell about the fire, the red floortiles, the
cupboard where lavender-water was kept, about candied
lilies and the soul of bread . . .

Jean Joubert
France
Translated by Denise Levertov

REMEMBERING
(excerpt from a longer poem)

My mouth is a horse's mouth—
language my hay, dried in sun and air.
The feet of birds are buried under the hay,
lizards on one side building a nest.
Talking about them causes me an
animal pain that pierces my heart,
takes my hand, places it on the word
to find the spot from which feelers sprout.

Childhood! My poems a clean house,
the fields a ball rolling.
Mother's two baskets on a pole across her shoulder.
Over emerald leaves, rivers rush on.
Had I ever worn the anxious look I wear now?
Make my poems a rag to wipe with—wash here, wash there.
Make grating sounds—wrench here, wrench there.
Throw the books on the floor.
From a snowy sky remote from humanity,
snowflakes striking become soundless tears.
Had I ever tried to praise beauty?
My entire body glittering quicksilver,
my first song was in my youth.
My teeth shone then like the horns of a fawn,
in the pride of life, my smile unhidden.
I walked then
like water drawn up from a well.

Remembering! this conch shell.

Xue Di
China
Translated by Iona Cook and Keith Waldrop

SPARROW

Year we worked
My mother got sick
Year we ate
My mother, cured!
This year, mother is sick
That year, mother is cured
Shall we eat, or shall we save the seeds?
Shall we eat, or shall we save the seeds?

Ewondo-Beti—traditional folk poem
Cameroon
English version by Judith Gleason

TRANSFORMATIONS

My little son enters
the room and says
"you are a vulture
I am a mouse"

I put away my book
wings and claws
grow out of me

their ominous shadows
race on the walls
I am a vulture
he is a mouse

"you are a wolf
I am a goat"
I walk around the table
and am a wolf
windowpanes gleam
like fangs
in the dark

65

while he runs to his mother
safe
his head hidden in the warmth of her dress

Tadeusz Różewicz
Poland
Translated by Czesław Miłosz

SOUVENIR OF THE ANCIENT WORLD

Clara strolled in the garden with the children.
The sky was green over the grass,
the water was golden under the bridges,
other elements were blue and rose and orange,
a policeman smiled, bicycles passed,
a girl stepped onto the lawn to catch a bird,
the whole world—Germany, China—
    all was quiet around Clara.

The children looked at the sky: it was not forbidden.
Mouth, nose, eyes were open. There was no
    danger.
What Clara feared were the flu, the heat, the
    insects.
Clara feared missing the eleven o'clock trolley:
She waited for letters slow to arrive,
She couldn't always wear a new dress. But
    she strolled in the garden, in the morning!
They had gardens, they had mornings in those days!

Carlos Drummond de Andrade
Brazil
Translated by Mark Strand

INDUSTRIAL CHILDHOOD

My mother played us
Prokofiev's Peter and Wolf
when I was 3 in Hamilton
    she went off to work
leaving him to guard us.

In the morning she made cans.
In the evening she waited on tables
    and carried a milk bottle, broken, for
protection.

Left me to comfort
    you, older brother,
You understood why the
wolf was destroyed.

My mother read us
Fenimore Cooper
when I was 5 in Sudbury
    in the big bed.

I didn't understand the colours
    of leaves
knowing only the black shot slate
    outside the window
the lacy women
    who must have carried milk bottles, broken,
somewhere,
and the magic Indians who could
    do everything
but survive.

Sharon Stevenson
Canada

I WAS BORN IN JACINTO VERA

I was born in Jacinto Vera.
What a neighborhood was Jacinto Vera!
Ranch houses made of tin on the outside
and on the inside, scraps of wood.

At night white would run
white would race the moon.
And I would run after her
and I would fly after her.

Suddenly I would lose her,
then suddenly she would appear
among the houses made of tin
and on the inside, scraps of wood.

Oh moon, my white moon,
moon of Jacinto Vera.

Liber Falco
Uruguay
Translated by Teresa Anderson

WEIGHTS

In Memory of My Mother,
Miriam Murray née Arnall

Not owning a cart, my father
in the drought years was a bowing
green hut of cattle feed, moving,
or gasping under cream cans. No weight
would he let my mother carry.

Instead, she wielded handles
in the kitchen and dairy, singing often,
gave saucepan-boiled injections
with her ward-sister skill, nursed neighbours,
scorned gossips, ran committees.

She gave me her factual tone,
her facial bones, her will,
not her beautiful voice
but her straightness and her clarity.

I did not know back then
nor for many years what it was,
after me, she could not carry.

Les Murray
Australia

SMALL WANTS

Nothing happens now, except when
I begin to think of the times
when they used to happen.
When I looked forward to the four-anna coin
my mother gave me every day
and asked me to preserve for future use.
New clothes were bought for all three of us
three times a year
to make us presentable before
friends, relations and sympathetic neighbors.
On Sundays and other holidays
our uncle took us
to the rich Naya Sarak Market
in his black Morris Minor.
We ate crisp hot *vadas*
at Madhu Sahu's ramshackle restaurant
on Pilgrim Road (now lost
and perhaps forgotten by everyone
except by the three of us).
Small wants, but they used to matter.

Today, even as the early sun
filters into my room through
the delicate, handwoven Sambalpuri curtains,
I think of them—
old wants that seem to bother no one any longer.
Relaxing on the reed mat spread on our
sprawling verandah on the second floor,
I ask my good wife to bring tea,
watch our old milkman's son bring
my son's milk for the day,
listen to the tireless doorbell ring
for no reason at all.

The familiar postman delivers parcels
from the British Council Library
and the American Studies Research Center,
lengthy letters from my two brothers
and even their loyal wives.
Laxmi, our maidservant, arrives
with her smiling eight-year-old daughter
tugging at her borrowed saree.

I keep myself busy through the day
drinking "matchless Darjeeling tea,"
listening to words
that lost their edge years ago when
I first began writing the language
without a flaw.
I still hunt the places where
hot crisp *vadas* are believed to be served,
accompanied now by my wife
and rather reluctant four-year-old son.
I still write letters, though
each gets shorter than the one
written before.
And, as the long Indian day comes to its end,
my son, his lisping voice
sounding curious and far like the rustle of leaves
through midnight air,
asks me questions I cannot answer.

Bibhu Padhi
India

Note: *Vadas* are considered to be a delicacy in the southern part of India. *Vadas* can be described as very spicy lentil donuts.

BELIEVE IT OR NOT

Mother looms up on the prairie out there.

And the mountain's been moved south
by Mother, believe it or not.

Years and years have gone by since then,
yet for Mother I'm still as tiny

as a grain of mustard seed.

Nicolai Kantchev
Bulgaria
Translated by Jascha Kessler and Alexander Shurbanov

BROWNOUT

Rather unexpectedly, the lights went out
In the middle of my cousin's story.
He stopped talking,
All around us paralyzed
And we sat still, slighted,
Wanting the dark to explain its intrusion.
I rose and switched the flashlight on,
Detesting its strange brightness.
The room looked different this way, I said,
Showing up shadows which were not there before.
But my cousin said nothing, he turned to me
And stared—he, too, looked different,
And continued his story—it was different, too.
I shut off the light and all was still again.
We lay patiently in bed,
Waiting in the dark, wondering
What would happen next.

Tony Perez
Philippines

ATONG

I left Atong by the schoolyard
fence—
where he waved and waved
saying Bye bye Bye bye Bye bye.

I still don't know what it was
that filled his face with light that day—
it was for me
a shower of white flowers
when he smiled
and then a flight of sparrows
when he smiled again.

and when I turned to leave
I could not understand why I, his mother, was
like a fool, so overcome with joy.

Benilda S. Santos
Philippines
Translated by Ramón C. Sunico

Note: The name "Atong" is pronounced with a short "a" as in "atom," accent on the second
syllable.

ATONG AND HIS GOODBYE

It is no longer as it once was
when there was no end to his waving
to his trailing looks
until I turned the corner
toward the school's gate.

It is because five years have passed.

The short pants are gone.
Now his slacks
must always match
his shirt, tucked-in,
and, complete with sideburns, his hair
parted neatly at the right.

When I say
"Okay son. Goodbye,"
his standard reply's
a tight smile
an eyebrow's twitch
or sometimes
the slightest of nods.

Nothing remains of the old goodbyes.

And when this happens to the mother he leaves behind
the wind blows through her though there is no breeze.
Here in the car, everything spins
though my foot is on the brake.
And I shiver though the sun burns
fiercely on the streets.

Benilda S. Santos
Philippines
Translated by Ramón C. Sunico

FATHER AND SON

Here is not good enough
And he looks at me with reproach
But what can I do
I'm not about to offer excuses
So I let my silence speak
Finally he hugs me
As if he suddenly realizes
We have to get along
To come to an agreement
There is no one else
To deal with

And after a while
We both get to work
He collects
Old bus tickets
I fuss with words
Out of which I can whittle
My crutches and cane

Tomasz Jastrun
Poland
Translated by Daniel Bourne

PETRIFIED MINUTE

In the big room my father stands
in shirt-sleeves, before the wall-
mirror: slipped from his hand,
a stiff collar lies white on the
russet floor—
            sixty years aren't time
enough for me to bend down for it.

Zoltań Zelk
Hungary
Translated by Barbara Howes

COMPANION

I said, I won't read
Butterflies do not read
Rivers do not
Nor does the ocean
Even the stars do not read.

Mummy said, I read
Your grandpa reads
So does your father
And millions of other people
Why would you remain different?

I said, I would play
Play with the butterfly
And float paper boats in the stream
Stars would decorate them

Now Mummy is no more
Father is away
I am sick
I read and only read
Books are brooks to me.

Manjush Dasgupta
India
Translated by the poet

A PEARL

This pearl
was a gift of my grandmother—that great lady—
    to my mother
    and my mother gave it to me
And now I hand it on to you
The three of you and this pearl
Have in common
    simplicity and truth
I give it with my love
and with the fullness of heart
    you excel in
The girls of Arabia will soon grow
    to full stature
They will look about and say
"She has passed by this road"
and point to the place of sunrise
and the heart's direction.

Fawziyya Abu Khalid
Saudi Arabia
Translated by Salwa Jabsheh and John Heath-Stubbs

A NEW DRESS

I don't want a new dress, I said.
My mother plucked from her mouth ninetynine pins.
I suppose there are plenty, she said, *girls of ten
Who would be glad to have a new dress.*

Snip-snip. Snip-snip. The cold scissors
Ate quickly as my white rabbit round my arm.

She won't speak to me if I have a new dress!
My feet rattled on the kitchen floor.

How can I fit you if you won't stand still?

My tears made a map of Australia
On the sofa cushion; from the hot center
My friend's eyes flashed, fierce as embers.
She would not speak to me, perhaps never again.
She would paralyze me with one piercing look.

I'd rather have my friend than a new dress!

My mother wouldn't understand, my grownup mother
Whose grasshopper thimble winked at the sun
And whose laughter was made by small waves
Rearranging seashells on Australia's shore.

Ruth Dallas
New Zealand

VISTASP

He was praying before the lamp—
Petromax. I crept up from behind,
Caught him at his shoulders,
Heaved him up above my head.
When I put him down, turned him
Around, I saw his face: shocked,
Speechless, as though he were the very god
I had flung into the air; but also
A silent thumping joy
At the outrage.
Now the thing was an impulse—
Given thought I wouldn't do it—
I am no god-destroyer,
I have little against prayer,

But he would have to take account,
Accommodate the fact
Of being swung out of holiness
Into a meaningless motion,
An arc of time to trace
A future doubt.
Would my silly act have made him
A thinker?
Later he came to me, shy and merry:
"This evening when I am praying,"
he said,
"do it again."

Gieve Patel
India

Note: Vistasp is the cousin of the poet. At the time this incident occurred, Vistasp was about five and the poet eighteen.

80

POEM FOR MY SON

I seem to know all about you:
your time, your place, your name,
the clean Indian-wheat colour of your skin,
your unpolished words.
But I know that there are also sounds
that you do not know, shapes
that you wouldn't recognize.
For instance, the owl's lean dark cry,
or the sea at Puri
during a small moon's night.
And, at this hour, when
you are breathing so quietly
beside your mother,
I seem to hear a faraway whisper
that almost tells me
you're not mine.
I hear the owl's cry,
the gentle expanding roar
of the blue waters of Puri.
Never mind. I know where my night sleeps,
undisturbed by every sound and thought,
so peacefully.

Bibhu Padhi
India

AN APPOINTMENT

At dawn the milk truck's bell should be lightly
    ringing
Your eyes still misted by sleep—
Again the sun god has risen late
"Child, wake up!"—I am lying face down
    on your pillow
"Today let's take the laundry basket down
      to a clear summer stream where we'll bleach
      our memories clean.
Let's play the old game of changing places—
You be Mother and I'll be you. You go wash the clothes
    and I'll rest.

Sweetly surround me with fragrant shrubbery,
Little white flowers sprinkled on a tree.
Like the soapsuds made while washing clothes,
Reflected in a bubble, my laughing face
    a song.
All afternoon I calculated the numbers of leaves
    on three trees
Because they were the small square handkerchiefs
    you washed
And hung out to dry in the sun . . .

Otherwise we could also go to the shore
Where the willows have already released
    their soft, soft swings.
We could swing all the way from March to August . . ."

Chang Shiang-hua
Taiwan
Translated by Stephen L. Smith with Naomi Shihab Nye

THE FIRST SHOE

We put the shoe on him the first time this morning,
minute, stitched-together, a little jewel of leather,
a miracle of shoemaking, in the first choice of fashion,
on the flowerlike foot never before in bondage,
the first shoe ever on that small honey-sweet foot.

Little treasure, heart of the house, here you go tramping,
strike the sole like this on the ground stoutly,
hold the precious head pluckily, determined,
a man-baby you are in your walk and your bearing,
the height of my knee, and so soon to leave me!

You have a long road to travel before you,
and tying your shoe is only the first tying.

Máire Mhac an tSaoi
Ireland
Translated by Brendan O Hehir

GRANDMOTHER

I hadn't asked her much,
just how she felt,
and she told me all about her day,
and how she'd washed the sheets,
and how she could not understand
why the towel got so heavy
when it was wet.
She'd also sunned the mattresses,
such tired bones and so much to do,

and my eyes filled with tears
when I thought of how I was simply
going to say "Salaam" and walk away
and so many words would have been
trapped inside her.
I would have passed by as if
what lay between those bedclothes
was just old life
and not really my grandmother.

Sameeneh Shirazie
Pakistan

Note: "Salaam," meaning "peace," is often used as a greeting.

MY LIFE STORY

What shall I tell about my life?

a life of changes
a life of losing
remembering
eighteen years ago
a little child was born
surrounded by the love of family
so warm and tender
surrounded by mountains and rivers
so free and beautiful

But life was not easy
the dearest father passed away
and left a big scar in the child's head

She grew up with something missing in her
She had seen the people born and dying
        born from the war
            dying from guns and bombs

Sometimes she wished
she could do something
for herself and her people

But what could she do?

Nothing but watch and watch
for she is too small
only a sand in the big desert
no power
nothing at all

She is only herself
an ordinary person
carrying a dream
that seems so far, far, far away

The only thing she can do
is keep hoping
one day her dream will come true

God cannot be mean to her forever.

Lan Nguyen
Vietnam

THE MUSHROOM RIVER

That river is full of mushrooms
    really, Mother. On the current of the river in
    which you soaked your hands
    my past flows by. The child wearing a red jacket
    exposes his skin of daylight. Along the river's
    bank he picks mushrooms while carrying a basket
    of smiles
    Do not enter the dark and miserable forest. Mother

return to join with me in fairy tales
    hiding in your voice that wolf as grandma, exposing
    the teeth of day
    And dark again returns. Will my love be lost? Mother.
    My childhood, gone forever
    Your hands contain the river's voice which overflows
    my eyes
    Do not follow the lonely path of old age. Mother

Mushrooms. Butterflies radiant in your silver hair
    The light is on. Toward you I walk, along the river.
    The fairy-tale wolf will die someday. To collect
    sounds of beauty along the road, the child grinds
    teeth in the wolf's abstracted mouth
    memory sprouting as endless white floating mushrooms,
    carrying you these remaining years
    Go back to the room. Do not wait for me, standing
    in misery. Remember my poetry's words. I'll bring
    to you the songs from vast fields

I'll tell you about the mushroom river

Xue Di
China
Translated by Ping Wang and Gale Nelson

LETTER FROM MY SON

There's a kite stuck on the misted glass
of my window.
I noticed it this morning after waking
from a long dream filled with cactus,
desolate canyons, empty beaches . . .
faceless humans encircled me,
a narrow bridge slanted up
toward the sky.
I woke just after reaching
the last foothold of the half-built bridge
before it faded into a foggy void.

Here it's winter—
I haven't seen any kites in this sky.
My heart had been lost under layers of snow
when I saw the green kite of my little Shomik
stuck on the misted glass of my window.

Once this kite was warm,
smelling of tropical sun,
green fields in afternoons,
the rain-soaked earth that mirrors
the first smiles of newborns.

I took a closer look at the kite.
Once it was tied to a long thread
quivering under soft pulls from the other end.
Suddenly my heart began to thaw,
frozen layers melting,
till I smelled the smell of my little Shomik
and saw him on the lawn at home,
flying a green kite.

Now it's stuck on the misted window.
Written on it in red, four words:
"PAPA, COME HOME SOON."

(Iowa City)
Shihab Sarkar
Bangladesh

SUMMER

Not yet.

Under the mango tree
the cold ash
of a deserted fire.

Who needs the future?

A ten-year-old girl
combs her mother's hair,
where crows of rivalries
are quietly nesting.

The home will never
be hers.

In a corner of her mind
a living green mango
drops softly to earth.

Jayanta Mahapatra
India

JASMINE

Saturday evening grows
darker as the teapot
whistles: I get a mug,
humming, and breathe
the ancient scent,
faintly familiar.

Every summer we
gathered the young
jasmine leaves, while I sang
songs that I learned in school.
On sunny days, she spread
the leaves out in the back
yard where I sat and dreamt
the scent of long winter
nights beside the hot stove.
Immense warmth calms my throat

as I hear
what's not there anymore.
Mama's dead: someone else
is picking the leaves,
drinking my tea
in nights of winter.

Kyongjoo Hong Ryou
South Korea

FOOTPATH

Path-let . . . leaving home, leading out,
Return my mother to me.
The sun is sinking and darkness coming,
Hens and cocks are already inside and babies drowsing,
Return my mother to me.
We do not have fire-wood and I have not seen the lantern,
There is no more food and the water has run out.
Path-let I pray you, return my mother to me.
Path of the hillocks, path of the small stones,
Path of slipperiness, path of the mud,
Return my mother to me.
Path of the papyrus, path of the rivers,
Path of the small forests, path of the reeds,
Return my mother to me.
Path that winds, path of the short-cut,
Over-trodden path, newly-made path,
Return my mother to me.
Path, I implore you, return my mother to me.
Path of the crossways, path that branches off,
Path of the stinging shrubs, path of the bridge,
Return my mother to me.
Path of the open, path of the valley,
Path of the steep climb, path of the downward slope,
Return my mother to me.
Children are drowsing about to sleep,
Darkness is coming and there is no fire-wood,
And I have not yet found the lantern:
Return my mother to me.

Stella Ngatho
Kenya

FAMILY PORTRAIT

I am like Jojon, the farmhand from Tegal
Who left his wife and two children behind
To pedal a pedicab in Jakarta.
Like Salka, the fisherman in Cilincing
Separated from his family on Madura Island.
Every three months or twice a year
We meet our wives and children, to free ourselves from longing.

I am a contract coolie, far from the family.
That is common, sir, common. Very common.
We are the hundreds of thousands of coolies
at the city's construction sites
Who have left our families behind in the village.
When looking at the clouds in the bright sky,
We do not cry, but neither are we delighted.
White clouds that pass over my village,
Tell them my life in the city's alright.

I'm just Jojon, on contract in London.
You and the children live quietly in the village.
When you see the mist descend from the sky,
Or when it rains for days before Christmas,
Relax, sleep in peace.
In your dreams I will send millions of stars,
As long as you, in your prayers, also mention my name.

Eka Budianta
Indonesia
Translated by E. U. Kratz

THIS EARTH AND SKY
IN WHICH WE LIVE

"Water That Used to Be a Cloud"

MINDORO

The sun dissolves:
some pieces float
on the green sea
which hurries to darkness.

The blood light flickers
while sporadically
a wave
slaps against the side of our slippery boat.

The red threads
of last-light
dance
on the shoulders of our oarsman.

No one notices
the stars
begin
to cluster like mayflies.

The call
of land
to us
is sharper than a fishhook:
the rented
home
and dinner steaming.

We are
all mutes
riding along on this boat.

To the left
the sea
slices the afternoon in two.

To the right
the mountains of Mindoro ripen.

Ramón C. Sunico
Philippines
Translated by the poet

Note: Mindoro is a well-known island with lovely coves and beaches in the Philippines.

DAWN

I kindle my light over the whole Atlantic . . .
Unknown worlds, night-covered lands
awaken toward me!
I am the cold dawn.
I am the pitiless goddess of the day
in misty grey veils
with a little early morning helmet-glitter.
Swiftly, swiftly my winds skim over the ocean.
My shiny horn hangs by my side,
I do not blow it for departure . . .
Do I still tarry? Is some god still dozing?
Morning rises red out of the ocean.

Edith Södergran
Sweden and Finland
Translated by Daisy Aldan with Leif Sjöberg

GRASS

The grass is strangely tall to me,
lying with my nose to the earth.
If I bow down as low as I can
my world grows high.

Under the pointed greenish gates
I stop. Here I shall stay.
I dare not lose my way
in the shining dark!
I dare not lose
my way among straw!

Inside the dawning halls of the straws
there is a voice waking, calling
in rising notes: comest thou now,
comest thou, comest thou, comest thou now,
thou now.

And as answer
sounds a bright
full of delight boyish bright voice in me:
No, oh not yet! No, oh not yet!
But when my madness is gone,
when my dreams of greatness are gone,
then I shall come, then I shall come,
then I'll be small and happy enough.

Tom Kristensen
Denmark
Translated by Poul Borum

THE LAND OF MISTS

In the land of mists
always shrouded in mist
nothing ever happens
And if something happens
nothing can be seen
because of the mist
for if you live in mist
you get accustomed to mist
so you don't try to see
Therefore in the land of mists
you should not try to see
you have to hear things
for if you don't hear you can't live
so ears keep on growing
People like rabbits
with ears of white mist
live in the land of mists

Kwang-kyu Kim
South Korea
Translated by Brother Anthony

SPRING POEM

HEARING: hearing: hearing:
The Engine warming up: warming
And the Earthworm going zupzupzup through the brown
    ground
Chased by that same hot crank.
Through the tunnelled air trundle the marvellous merry
    birds:
All carrying rich pokes, wearing super stoles
And showing off the fine detail of freckles on their tails; just
    as clearly
As the big block: the elephant block: the big E
Of my mammoth city shows its grim windows and dopey
    blinds.
O the Engine: the Elevator: of me and mind:
It goes down its stretchy rubber cables:
Capable or incapable:
But going zupzupzup.

Colleen Thibaudeau
Canada

DEW
—Lake Bratan, Bali

Dew adorns the morning world
Dew sets our senses shivering
Dewdrops of thought and feeling
The layer of dew upon the land
simmers beneath the silent sun

Dewdrops drip like falling tears
Dewdrops, the manifold plans of distant men
Oh, how the heat and the dew of this world
become the body's steam and drops of sweat

Linus Suryadi AG
Indonesia
Translated by John H. McGlynn

beside a stone three
thousand years old: two
red poppies of today

Christine M. Krishnasami
India

COUNTRY MEMORY
(At Pina's House)
for Iván

At Pina's house
there was a garden with a swing
I soared too high for my age
and a wide passageway
where my parents
built up mountains of corncobs
from the other side of the hedge
the neighbor's son spied on us
Pina and I would swing
my dresses were made at home
by my mother and a sewing machine
our skirts flew
and I pumped harder
to clear the hedge
and play tag and chase
in the neighbor's garden
soiling my dresses
on the other side of the hedge

Leticia Herrera Alvarez
Mexico
Translated by Judith Infante

CUERNAVACA

There's a deep murmur unravelled,
the air is a song of feather,
a soft babble of grass.
There's a memory of heaven revived,
hum of life and a plea.
There's this need, like a baby's, to be loved.

Aline Pettersson
Mexico
Translated by Judith Infante

MOUNTAIN TAMBOURINE

A crew took part of the big tree away
on my street. A poplar, it was throwing
its ashes, its dirty pillow stuffing,
around too much. So they said. Anyway,
people were tired of it. It was too grey.
It might drop a tired branch and hit something,
a power or phone line. What's still standing
they'll come for tomorrow and chop away.
It doesn't make much poplar talk now. The big
clatter's gone out of it. On the older
side of the street, the last tree stands, tall, big,
full, leafy—a fine shade and rain holder.
It leans to one side at a warm angle,
like Annie, whose door it covered last fall.

Peter van Toorn
Canada

The sodden moss sinks underfoot when we cross half-frozen bays and walk through birch groves, wandering in an uneven circle that widens into darkness, through the minds and bodies of men and animals trapped in last year's snow—no: trapped from the beginning, emptiness all around us, ice collecting on our pale faces, I can hear you singing on the run, an unknown melody, I can't make out the words, clouds of breath freeze on your fur collar, eyes open wide as we trudge through silence and weakening starlight, through the fevered babble of children exiled to distant camps, insects curling up under bark, December or June, no difference, ashes blanket the ground as far as you can see, damp wool of shirts, we wade through the fog rolling in from the hills, oozing into our lungs, hills where there must be flowers about to bloom under a woman's eyelids, who dreams of dark faces hardening into granite, the snow's covering us, we're asleep on our feet, under the steel-gray sky, oblivious to the rhythms of sunrise and sunset, endless, as if they never began, our teeth crack in the cold, we don't want to separate, I can barely swallow, tell me the lyrics of your song, I want to sing with you.

Aleš Debeljak
Slovenia
Translated by Christopher Merrill

IMPROVISATION (ECHING)

In the drizzle
the tractor pulls
the sea-gulls
in its wake
along a wet, black field.
The furrows, pleats
opened by the plough,
catch the light like waves.
One by one, the birds sheer
off abruptly,
but return to their place
in the sky, held there
like children's kites.

Kevin Perryman
Bavaria

Note: Eching is a village in southern Germany.

Greedy snowslide
keep your paws off my little house
I've got a wife and four kids
they could never gratify you
like they gratify me

Strong snowslide
if you must flex your muscles
kindly smash a few rocks
bury a cliff-side or two
but don't touch this little house of mine

I know, O snowslide
that I built my house on your land
but where else could I find shelter
from your comrade the wind?
Where else but in your lap?

Generous snowslide
my wife and kids are all I have
it wouldn't amuse you to kill them
let them sleep in peace
Stay up there on your nice cold mountain

East Greenland—traditional song
Greenland
Translated by Lawrence Millman

THE SKY IS VAST

Once in this vast sky
lived a tiny cloud
a tiny solitary cloud
many vast clouds moving around it

The little cloud was tearful
He said, "How great are those clouds!
They will crumple me, let me hide!
I am so small, they will crush me!"

The tiny cloud drifted
Many clouds laughed at it
and said, "See how ugly it is"

The tiny cloud cried
and looked for its mother
"Oh Mama, come soon,
the giants are coming!"

The mother cloud heard the
child's voice

Fast she came and they merged
into one

The sun was behind them
as they rolled forward

The sun smiled at the little cloud
and the little cloud blushed in the vast sky

Pramila Khadun
Mauritius
Translated by the poet

THE PENGUIN
To J. E. and of course, J. E. P.

The penguin isn't meat, fish or bird,
doesn't belong to carnival or Lent.
Least attractive animal, and most mysterious,
he splashes in the three elements, and has
some rudimentary right over them all, but yet
he feels uneasy with them:
on soil he limps
      in water he moves by sculling
           and on air
he flaps and falls down.
As if she herself felt strange about him,
nature hides him
in the frontier of the world.

Ricardo Yáñez
Mexico
Translated by Raúl Aceves and
Arturo Súarez with Jane Taylor

THE OPEN SHUTTER

Someone pouring light
Out of the window.
The roses of air
Open.
And children
Playing in the street
Look up.
Pigeons nibble
At its sweetness.
Girls are beautiful
And men gentle
In this light.
But before the others say so
Someone shuts
The window again.

Karl Krolow
Germany
Translated by Kevin Perryman

WIND'S FOAM

Nothing remains, see, leaves, flowers, village elders,
the river's dancing waves, brass pitchers and the hookah's coal;
groups of growing girls one by one dwindle like the *ilish* season,
yellow leaves in the wind on the rainless fields and meadows
        drop rustling. The migrant geese go too,
their bodies like multitudinous bubbles
      in the sky's blue cup.

Why does nothing remain? Corrugated iron, thatch or mud walls,
the ageless village *bat* tree are uprooted in the terrible
        Chittagong typhoon.
Plaster cracks; as vast as faith,
with a great crash, finally
      crumbles and falls the local mosque.

Sparrows' nests, love, creepers' leaves, book covers
fall torn and twisted. Bitten by the Meghna's waters
the harvest's green cry shivers to the horizon
Houses, water-pitchers, cowsheds float,
and an old pillow, flower-embroidered, sinks like childish affection.
After this, not a dwelling remains;
water-loving birds fly, wiping the wind's foam from their beaks.

Al Mahmud
Bangladesh
Translated by Marian Maddern

Notes: This silver hilsa or *ilish* is a very tasty fish found in the rivers of Bangladesh. The rainy season is the best time for catching these fish, and so the season has been termed the ilish season.

The *bat* tree is the big banyan tree, which spreads its branches widely. The shade of the banyan tree is nice and cool.

The Meghna River starts in the Himalaya mountains and runs through India and into Bangladesh. The river is deep, wide and very swift.

THE SQUIRREL

The first hazelnut trundles down from above.
The second hazelnut, the third, the fourth, the fifth, and
the sixth, trundle down from above.
The hazelnuts trundle down, nut by nut, to the ground beneath
the dumb tree, the tree whose memory the squirrel collects
nut by nut, rolling it into his den.
Each year a memory of hazelnuts rolls, nut by nut, into
the den of the prince with the merry tail,
and the tree forgets.

Saleem Barakat
Syria
Translated by Lena Jayyusi and Naomi Shihab Nye

THE BIRTH OF A STONE

In those deep mountain ravines
I wonder if there are stones
that no one has ever visited?
I went up the mountain
in quest of a stone no one had ever seen
from the remotest of times

Under ancient pines
on steep pathless slopes
there was a stone
I wonder
how long
this stone all thick with moss
has been
here?

Two thousand years? Two million? Two billion?
No
Not at all
If really till now no one
has ever seen this stone
it is only
here
from now on
This stone
was only born
the moment I first saw it

Kwang-kyu Kim
South Korea
Translated by Brother Anthony

CARING FOR ANIMALS

I ask sometimes why these small animals
With bitter eyes, why we should care for them.

I question the sky, the serene blue water,
But it cannot say. It gives no answer.

And no answer releases in my head
A procession of gray shades patched and whimpering,

Dogs with clipped ears, wheezing cart horses
A fly without shadow and without thought.

Is it with these menaces to our vision
With this procession led by a man carrying wood

We must be concerned? The holy land, the rearing
Green island should be kindlier than this.

Yet the animals, our ghosts, need tending to.
Take in the whipped cat and the blinded owl;

Take up the man-trapped squirrel upon your shoulder.
Attend to the unnecessary beasts.

From growing mercy and a moderate love
Great love for the human animal occurs.

And your love grows. Your great love grows and grows.

Jon Silkin
England

AUTUMN AND THE SEA

With autumn coming in,
I go down to the sea and look for golden shells,
they lie like leaves,
the ocean casts them up precipitously
on the sand,
and in between the waves,
and while the sea runs off and edges back,
the white scales of the fish
(shed at the sound of the autumn wind
that reaches to the bottom of the ocean)
appear, ready to be gathered in by hand.

White shells,
I still can hear the ocean sounds
I used to hear when childhood
was small and sweet
I still can hear, within the depths
of every sleeping shell,
the vast sea-roar!

They lie like leaves,
fallen to the bottom of the ocean.
The ocean moves them and renews them,
beats against them, smashes them
and barefoot autumn hands them over,
gathering them in and shoving them away.

Javier Heraud
Peru
Translated by Naomi Lindstrom

PITCHER

Fragrant roundness
of earth cooked again
with a plate on its mouth
and a jar upside down.

In a clay bud
the water falls asleep,
captured and pure
for my acid thirst.

What a brown modesty
in your curves
anointed by two tanned hands
stained your same color.

Pitcher retaining
in terrestrial breast
with sober simplicity
a taste of sleepy water,

Between your lips sings
your liquid freshness,
the clear sound
of such roundness.

Renée Ferrer de Arréllaga
Paraguay
Translated by Raquel Chaves with Naomi Shihab Nye

CLEANED THE CROCODILE'S TEETH

His head is so white it shines,
it shines like bird's wood.
Oh, white ox with your shining head!

I danced at the cattlecamp of a girl with teeth.
I crossed the river to dance,
to dance at the deer pasture.

There I found a leech dancing like this
and a lou snake winding downriver.
I fixed its hair with an acacia thorn,
then we compared hairdos.

I found a lion pursuing people.
I sharpened the buffalo's horns
but I didn't dawdle. I sat on the deer's horn
and cleaned the crocodile's teeth with sand.
Then I flossed the elephant's teeth with grass.

A lou snake is as tough as python.
I cooked one with rice grass.
A frog escaped.

Sung by Nyabuk Col
Nuerland, Africa
Translated by Terese Svoboda

Notes: The lou snake is believed to have long hair and blue markings, and to live in the river.

Children in Nuerland have their permanent incisor teeth removed—Nuer people believe a full set of teeth makes a person look like a hyena.

The Nuer people live in the southern Sudan along the Nile near the Ethiopian border. There is no place called Nuerland on any map.

CAT

Again and again through the day
I meet a cat.
In the tree's shade, in the sun, in the crowding brown leaves
After the success of a few fish bones
Or inside a skeleton of white earth
I find it, as absorbed in the purring
Of its own heart as a bee.
Still it sharpens its claws on the *gulmohar* tree
And follows the sun all day long.

Now I see it and then it is gone,
Losing itself somewhere.
On an autumn evening I have watched it play,
Stroking the soft body of the saffron sun
With a white paw. Then it caught
The darkness in paws like small balls
And scattered it all over the earth.

Jibananda Das
India
Translated by Lila Ray

THE MOON RISES SLOWLY OVER THE OCEAN

It is time
We stand like children
On the silent beach
And calmly wait for the moon
Nothing has been lost on the moon today
A banana kazoo
Sucked between the lips of night
Is no longer blowing out of tune

Crisscrossed boughs set up an easel
The moon wearing a pure white suncap
Slowly comes over like a shy boy
Holding a transparent nylon net
With which to scavenge the ocean
Of its many broken hearts
Bobbing on the sea to the horizon

Xu De-min
China
Translated by Edward Morin and Dennis Ding

STARS AT NIGHT

There are stars above Japan.
There are stars that smell of gasoline.
There are stars that have heavy accents.
There are stars that sound like Ford automobiles.
There are stars that are Coca-Cola colored.
There are stars that have the humming of electric
    refrigerators.
There are stars that contain the rattling of cans.

Cleaned out with gauze and pincers
there are stars disinfected with formalin.
There are stars that hold radioactivity.
Among the stars are some too quick to catch with the eyes.
Stars that run along unexpected orbits.
Deeply, deeply,
stars are seen too that thrust into the gorge-bottom of the
    universe.

There are stars up above Japan.
They, on a winter's night,
each night, each night,
are seen linked like heavy chains.

Iku Takenaka
Japan
Translated by Edith Marcombe Shiffert and Yūki Sawa

THE PIT PONIES

They come like the ghosts of horses, shyly,
To this summer field, this fresh green,
Which scares them.

They have been too long in the blind mine,
Their hooves have trodden only stones
And the soft, thick dust of fine coal,

And they do not understand the grass.
For over two years their sun
Has shone from an electric bulb

That has never set, and their walking
Has been along the one, monotonous
Track of the pulled coal-trucks.

They have bunched their muscles against
The harness and pulled, and hauled.
But now they have come out of the underworld

And are set down in the sun and real air,
Which are strange to them. They are humble
And modest, their heads are downcast, they

Do not expect to see very far. But one
Is attempting a clumsy gallop. It is
Something he could do when he was very young,

When he was a little foal a long time ago
And he could run fleetly on his long foal's legs,
And almost he can remember this. And look,

One rolls on her back with joy in the clean grass!
And they all, awkwardly and hesitantly, like
Clumsy old men, begin to run, and the field

Is full of happy thunder. They toss their heads,
Their manes fly, they are galloping in freedom.
The ponies have come above ground, they are galloping!

Leslie Norris
Wales

Note: Ponies and donkeys were used in mines to pull carts of ore—in the United States
as well as Great Britain.

GREAT ASO

Horses are standing in rain.
A herd of horses with one or two foals is standing in rain.
In hushed silence rain is falling.
The horses are eating grass.
With tails, and backs too, and manes too, completely
    soaking wet
they are eating grass,
eating grass.
Some of them are standing with necks bowed over absent-
    mindedly and not eating grass.
Rain is falling and falling in hushed silence.
The mountain is sending up smoke.
The peak of Nakadake is sending up dimly yellowish and
    heavily oppressive volcanic smoke, densely, densely.
And rain clouds too all over the sky.
Still they continue without ending.
Horses are eating grass.
On one of the hills of the Thousand-Mile-Shore-of-Grass
they are absorbedly eating blue-green grass.
Eating.
They are all standing there quietly.
They are quietly gathered in one place forever, dripping
    and soaked with rain.
If a hundred years go by in this single moment, there would
    be no wonder.
Rain is falling. Rain is falling.
In hushed silence rain is falling.

Tatsuji Miyoshi
Japan
Translated by Edith Marcombe Shiffert and Yūki Sawa

Note: Great Aso is the name of a volcanic crater.

ANTS

A thread of red ants
moves between the door and my bed
I rise from sleep and grope
then crush the ants
and sleep again and wake
         to find the thread
of red ants between bed
and door has grown
to a thick rope

Yusuf al-Sa'igh
Iraq
Translated by Diana Der Hovanessian with Salma Khadra Jayyusi

FROM *DIARY OF A WOODCUTTER*

Wrinkles in the lake
and in the body,

wrinkles in the stones
and in memory,

wrinkles in September
and in leaves of the air,

wrinkles in the rain
falling on everything

in a time of wrinkles.

Into the lake the sky slides,
into the sky the lake slides,
into the lake and the sky the world slides,
the air shatters,
and on the surface darkness floats.

For the source, it takes time to reach the sea,
for the star, it takes time to touch the eye,
for the wind, it takes time to rock the boat,
and for the land, it takes time to reap the harvest.
Time ripens slowly under the crust,
and suddenly the summer sun
and the grapes.

An old pool,
grass at the bottom
where a fish plays.
It plays in the water that used to be a cloud,
in the cloud that used to be water,
the whole day that used to be night,
the whole night that used to be day.

Fuad Rifka
Lebanon
Translated by the poet and Shirley Kaufman

UNDER THIS SKY

There's an enormous comfort knowing
we all live under this same sky,
whether in New York or Dhaka,
we see the same sun and same moon.

When it is night in New York,
the sun shines in Dhaka,
but that doesn't matter.
Flowers that blossom here in spring
are unknown in meadows of distant Bengal—
that too doesn't matter.
There's no rainy season here—
the peasant in Bengal welcomes the new crop
with homemade sweets
while here, winter brings mountains of snow.

No one here knows Grandmother's hand-sewn quilt—
even that doesn't matter.
There's an enormous comfort knowing
we all live under this same sky.

The Hudson River freezes,
automobiles can't move.
Slowly city workers will remove the snow.
The old lady next door won't go to work—
it's too cold.
Maybe my old mother far away
will also enter her kitchen late.
Naked trees in Central Park and Ramna Park
quiver with dreams of new life and love.

Fog hangs on the horizon—
suddenly New York, Broadway, and Times Square
look dimly like Dhaka, Buriganga, and Laxmi Bazaar.

Zia Hyder
Bangladesh
Translated by Bhabani Sengupta with Naomi Shihab Nye

LOSSES

"Kissed Trees"

What is it that upsets the volcanoes
that spit fire, cold and rage?

Why wasn't Christopher Columbus
able to discover Spain?

How many questions does a cat have?

Do tears not yet spilled
wait in small lakes?

Or are they invisible rivers
that run toward sadness?

Pablo Neruda
Chile
Translated by William O'Daly

THERE'S AN ORANGE TREE OUT THERE

There's an orange tree out there, behind that old,
abandoned garden wall,
but it's not the same orange tree we planted,
and it's a beautiful orange tree
so beautiful it makes us remember
that orange tree we planted

                              —in our earth—

before coming to this house
so distant and remote from that one
where we planted an orange tree
and even saw it—like this one—in flower.

Alfonso Quijada Urías
El Salvador
Translated by Darwin J. Flakoll

HORSE BY MOONLIGHT
For Juan Soriano

A horse escaped from the circus
and lodged in my daughter's eyes:
there he ran circles around the iris
raising silver dust-clouds in the pupil
and halting sometimes
to drink from the holy water of the retina.

Since then my daughter feels a longing
for meadows of grass and green hills . . .

waiting for the moon to come
and dry with its silk sleeves
the sad water that wets her cheeks.

Alberto Blanco
Mexico
Translated by Jennifer Clement

A TREE

A tree
has been felled

Its leaves
are still alive
its fruits
are still ripening
and birds
are still on its branches

A tree
has been felled

Klara Koettner-Benigni
Austria
Translated by Herbert Kuhner

LOVE

I believed:
a tree when kissed
would not lose its leaves—
leaves fall
from kissed
trees.

A river hugged
by a hand in love
would not flow away—
it flows away
into fog.

There are in my landscape
errors of colors and scents
yet always
always I love
what incessantly
changes.

As a golden ball
she runs before me:
approached again and again,
my beloved,
Earth.

Tymoteusz Karpowicz
Poland
Translated by Czesław Miłosz

A BRIEF NOTE TO THE BAG LADY, MA SISTER
to Felicia Campbell

Ma sister, ma sister
Maybe lady maybe not
I'm sorry, I'm sorry for you
But I know it's not enough
'Cause I know not enough
Ma sister, no not enough

I'm sitting in a coffee house
Watching TV, waiting
All I know ma sister
You know nothin' 'bout me
You dunno nothin' 'bout the cold here
Here's no 5th Avenue
Here's no Central Park
Here's no Statue of Liberty
The cold here ma sister
Don't take place on your TV channels
God knows how many
Here is South-East Asia Minor
Now is winter
The avalanches at −42° C
Are not as minor

First came when I was out to find the doctor
On my way back I couldn't find
I couldn't find ma house under the snows
TV news says a second swallowed the whole village
No house is as tall as the twin towers
Here nothing's new, no york is new york here
I worked and worked all ma life ma sister
Now I have no belongings but here
Here ma sister you can find bags everywhere
Plastic bags, nylon bags, bags made of *kilims*
I don't know what to put in them
Maybe my freezing heart, maybe not

I'm watching you here ma sister
Here's no Brooklyn Bridge
Here's no bridge ma sister
Soon will be spring
The Flood will sweep the left-overs
Then I will never find ma children
Noah won't visit us I know
He wouldn't let me in, ma sister
He'd be disappointed here
'Cause here's so many lonely souls
So many women, husbands'n children gone
Ma sister, thank God you have some belongings
Belongings to carry in your bag, you have them
You have them and that makes you a lady
And to the streets yes to the streets maybe
You belong, but maybe not.

Ma sister, ma sister
I'm no lady whether I have a bag or not
Here is no lady, no lady am I
I'm in a coffee house waiting
They haven't found ma home yet
I'm sitting in a coffee house watching
I'm watching you and your old bag in new york

They tell me they will give me
Lots of money, God knows how money
How money would touch ma identity
They say I will have a new house
I dunno where, they don't see I lost ma home
They say I will have a TV-set
So many channels, so many other worlds
I'm watching yours now, by a stove
I can touch the stove, I put ma hands on it
Cold metal burns ma hands
I can't move nowhere, I can't talk to no one
They'll find ma house soon
And get ma dark-skinned, emerald-eyed

Emerald-eyed and rosy-cheeked buds out of the snow
Ma sister, the snow is everywhere
Ma sister, how will they do it?
Ma sister, I could do it better
With ma nails ma sister
I could do it better
But they wouldn't let me, no they wouldn't let me

Ma sister, I see your life is tough too
In the middle of so much plenty
You are hungry
I don't remember eating for days
I dunno, I really dunno
I'm watching you here in the avalanche area
Here is South-East Asia Minor, Anatolia, winter
It's eight to the twenty-first century
I'm watching you on TV ma sister
You're cold in the streets I see
Your heart may be freezing too, maybe not, dunno

I see, I see ma sister, you have no home
I see, you're cold and hungry
But still I can't be sorry enough
I'm sorry ma sister, but I can't
I can't be sorry enough.

Yusuf Eradam
Turkey

Note: Kilims are traditional and very beautiful Turkish rugs.

A MAN NEVER CRIES

I used to believe that story
that a man never cries.

And I used to think I was a man.

In my youth
I dared not be a coward
when we played our arrogant games of childhood
imitating the heroic man of steel in the movies.

Now I tremble
And now I cry.

As a man trembles.
As a man cries!

José Craveirinha
Mozambique
Translated by Don Burness

SURPRISE
For Luisa

A balloon! My Daddy brought for me
and it is like my Mama's belly,
and the cord and my arm are one:
      it goes up, I go up,
      I go down, it goes down.
I am the hummingbird awed
by that highest rosebud.
Oh my balloon, where may it be?
It hangs like a wrinkled wing
from the highest thorn of the tree
and the ground bruises and bruises my knees.

Blanca Rodriguez
Mexico
Translated by Aurelio Major

"OH! OH! SHOULD THEY TAKE AWAY MY STOVE . . ." MY INEXHAUSTIBLE ODE TO JOY

I have a stove
like a triumphal arch!

They're taking away my stove
like a triumphal arch!!

Give me back my stove
like a triumphal arch!!!

They took it away.
All that's left
       is a grey
           gaping
               hole
       a grey gaping hole.

And that's enough for me:
grey gaping hole
grey-gaping-hole
grey-ga-ping-hole
greygapinghole.

Miron Bialoszewski
Poland
Translated by Andrzej Busza and Bogdan Czaykowski

A TRAIN IS PASSING

A train is passing
a whistle sounds
stop   stop   the trees cry
but it's no use
a train is passing
a sound expires
stop life cries
we   are   already   far   away

Poul Borum
Denmark
Translated by the poet

A GIFT HORSE

Somebody must have
given it to someone;
only gifts and toys
can suffer

such love, such neglect,
soaked
in the wetness
of this lawn.

Cloth, or perhaps wood,
it is only that.
The hard and soft,
it's all the same.

Its owner,
the child, must be
asleep or have
found something else.

I am unable
to make out
its beginnings
or end exactly:

the eyes are a bleary
black;
the mouth seems sealed
airtight

as if to lock out
a couple of proverbs.
I do not think
it will speak.

Alamgir Hashmi
Pakistan

IN THE LEBANESE MOUNTAINS

Remember—the noise of moonlight
when the summer night collides with a peak
and traps the wind
in the rocky caves of the mountains of Lebanon.

Remember—a town on a sheer cliff
set like a tear on the rim of an eyelid,
one discovers there a pomegranate tree
and rivers more sonorous
than a piano.

Remember—the grapevine under the fig tree,
the cracked oak that September waters,
fountains and muleteers,
the sun dissolving in the river currents.

Remember—basil and apple tree,
mulberry syrup and almond groves.
Each girl was a swallow then
whose eyes moved like a gondola
swung from a hazel branch.

Remember—the hermit and goatherd,
paths that rise to the edge of a cloud,
the chant of Islam, crusaders' castles,
and wild bells ringing through July.

Remember—each one, everyone,
storyteller, prophet and baker,
the words of the feast and the words of the storm,
the sea shining like a medal in the landscape.

Remember—the child's recollection
of a secret kingdom just our age.
We did not know how to read the omens
in those dead birds in the bottoms of their cages,
in the mountains of Lebanon.

Nadia Tueni
Lebanon
Translated by Samuel Hazo

THE GARDEN OF A CHILD

I entered the garden of my childhood days after
the storm had passed over. A gentle breeze was
blowing and the sky was blue. Seeing in the
undergrowth a bird that had come out of an egg
only a little while ago and had fallen down, I
put it back in its nest.
It all happened yesterday. Today I am a grown-up
man again, and I just can't put anything back in
its proper place.

Nirendranath Chakravarti
India
Translated by the poet

BICYCLES
For V. Bokov

The bicycles lie
In the woods, in the dew.
    Between the birch trees
    The highroad gleams.

They fell, fell down
Mudguard to mudguard,
    Handlebar to handlebar
    Pedal to pedal.

And you can't
Wake them up!
    Petrified monsters,
    Their chains entwined.

Huge and surprised
They stare at the sky.
    Above them, green dusk
    Resin, and bumblebees.

In the luxurious
Rustling of camomile, peppermint
    Leaves they lie. Forgotten,
    Asleep. Asleep.

Andrei Voznesensky
Russia
Translated by Anselm Hollo

THE MEMORY OF HORSES

The lines in old people's hands
bend over slowly and soon point toward the earth.
They take their secret language there with them,
words from the clouds and letters from the winds,
all the signs the heart gathers up in impoverished years.

Sorrow bleaches out and turns to the stars
but the memory of horses, women's feet, children
streams from their faces into the grass's kingdom.

In large trees we can often picture
the calm of animal flanks,
and the wind draws in the grass, if you are happy,
running children and horses.

Rolf Jacobsen
Norway
Translated by Roger Greenwald

INSIDE

It hurts, the things of old,
attachment to the things of old.

Let go of them,
let them go as they are;
from afar comes the sound of
the scissors of the rag-picker.

Kim Chiha
South Korea
Translated by Kim Uchang

Note: The rag collectors make noise with their scissors as they walk around neighborhoods looking for rubbish and rags to be collected and salvaged.

HOME

Between the sunset and the eucalyptus tree
Paint peeling walls. The windows gleaming red,
Lights in the bedrooms. Hibiscus, quisquailis,
and dry earth moistened.
The thrum of summer insects,
The ark-ark of frogs,
Hushed brushed wings of sleepy birds,
Echoes barking, distant dogs,
The new night comes
Chairs on the lawn.
Veranda doors wide open,
A stillness rising to the stars.
What stillness over house
and childhood garden.
Grief grips my throat. I must go on
Over the vanished years, into the empty room,
Come back, come back, come back and be
Between the dark night and the eucalyptus tree.

Nasima Aziz
India

BEFORE THE GAME

Shut one eye then the other
Peek into every corner of yourself
See that there are no nails no thieves
See that there are no cuckoo's eggs

Shut then the other eye
Squat and jump
Jump high high high
On top of yourself

Fall then with all your weight
Fall for days on end deep deep deep
To the bottom of your abyss

Who doesn't break into pieces
Who remains whole who gets up whole
Plays

Vasko Popa
Yugoslavia
Translated by Charles Simic

HUMAN MYSTERIES

"White Bracelets"

NAPOLEON

Children, when was
Napoleon Bonaparte
born? asks the teacher.

A thousand years ago, say the children.
A hundred years ago, say the children.
Nobody knows.

Children, what did
Napoleon Bonaparte
do? asks the teacher.

He won a war, say the children.
He lost a war, say the children.
Nobody knows.

Our butcher used to have a dog,
says Frankie,
and his name was Napoleon,
and the butcher used to beat him,
and the dog died
of hunger
a year ago.

And now all the children feel sorry
for Napoleon.

Miroslav Holub
Czechoslovakia
Translated by Kaca Polackova

LOCKED IN

All my life I lived in a coconut.
It was cramped and dark,
especially in the morning when I had to shave.
But what pained me most was that I had no way
to get in touch with the outside world.
If no one out there happened to find the coconut,
if no one cracked it, then I was doomed
to live all my life in the nut, and maybe even die there.
    I died in the coconut.
A couple of years later they found the coconut,
cracked it, and discovered me shrunk and crumpled inside.
    "What an accident!"
    "If only we had found it earlier . . ."
    "Then maybe we could have saved him."
    "Maybe there are more of them locked in like that,"
they said, and started knocking to pieces every coconut
within reach.
    No use! Meaningless! A waste of time!
A person who chooses to live in a coconut!
Such a person is one in a million!
      But I have a brother-in-law who
   lives in an
   acorn.

Ingemar Leckius
Sweden
Translated by May Swenson

DEBT

I used to drop my pocket money
into the rain grates by the road
taking them for piggy-banks—
that's why it's the sea
that owes me most

Sunay Akin
Turkey
Translated by Yusuf Eradam

A BOY'S HEAD

In it there is a space-ship
and a project
for doing away with piano lessons.

And there is
Noah's ark,
which shall be first.

And there is
an entirely new bird,
an entirely new hare,
an entirely new bumble-bee.

There is a river
that flows upwards.

There is a multiplication table.

There is anti-matter.

And it just cannot be trimmed.

I believe
that only what cannot be trimmed
is a head.

There is much promise
in the circumstance
that so many people have heads.

Miroslav Holub
Czechoslovakia
Translated by Ian Milner

THE SHIP'S WHISTLE

What's the hurry? The ship's not sailing till
Half past five; it's two now. Red leather suitcase,
Walking cane, umbrella, heavy bedding, at
This odd hour, why wait alone at the dock; wait
Here, this old broken house, many rooms; whether
You will return—who knows—so what's the hurry?

Look at that photo on the wall, you took that
Happily at a fair once, next to it a vase,
Your old paper flowers still in that vase
Forever fresh—forever, what does that mean?
A ship's whistle? A saffron sky at
Sunset?
        What's the hurry? No harm in waiting
A little.

Tarapada Ray
India
Translated by Shyamasree Devi and P. Lal

SWEET LIKE A CROW
for Hetti Corea, 8 *years old*

Your voice sounds like a scorpion being pushed
through a glass tube
like someone has just trod on a peacock
like wind howling in a coconut
like a rusty bible, like someone pulling barbed wire
across a stone courtyard, like a pig drowning,

a vattacka being fried
a bone shaking hands
a frog singing at Carnegie Hall.

Like a crow swimming in milk,
like a nose being hit by a mango
like the crowd at the Royal-Thomian match,
a womb full of twins, a pariah dog
with a magpie in its mouth
like the midnight jet from Casablanca
like Air Pakistan curry,
a typewriter on fire, like a hundred
pappadams being crunched, like someone
trying to light matches in a dark room,
the clicking sound of a reef when you put your head into the sea,
a dolphin reciting epic poetry to a sleepy audience,
the sound of a fan when someone throws brinjals at it,
like pineapples being sliced in the Pettah market
like betel juice hitting a butterfly in mid-air
like a whole village running naked onto the street
and tearing their sarongs, like an angry family
pushing a jeep out of the mud, like dirt on the needle,
like 8 sharks being carried on the back of a bicycle
like 3 old ladies locked in the lavatory
like the sound I heard when having an afternoon sleep
and someone walked through my room in ankle bracelets.

Michael Ondaatje
Canada

Note: A vattacka is a vegetable. Pappadams are extremely thin, crispy, round lentil wafers,
which can be dipped into various sauces. Brinjal is a British word for eggplant.

VOLUNTEER WORKER

The small ones wanted pieces of me.
I was big. They wanted pieces of me.
They pulled me apart.
There was no pain, and so I did not struggle.
"I want his eyes!" they said.
"I want his lips, I want his ears!"
"I want his hands!" they said.
There was much blood.
But thinking it charitable,
I offered myself.
They ate of me.

      After they had feasted,
I rose, and found I was as small as they.
They ran. I followed.
"Let me play with you!" I cried.
But they said they did not love me.

Tony Perez
Philippines

BEHIND BARS

My mother's phantom hovers here
her forehead shines before my eyes
like the light of stars
She might be thinking of me now,
dreaming

> (Before my arrest
> I drew letters in a book
> new and old
> I painted roses
> grown with blood
> and my mother was near me
> blessing my painting)

I see her
on her face silence and loneliness now
and in the house
silence and loneliness
My satchel there on the bookshelf
and my school uniform
on the hanger
I see her hand reaching out
brushing the dust from it
I follow my mother's steps
and listen to her thoughts
yearning for her arms and the face of day

Fadwa Tuqan
Palestine
Translated by Hatem Hussaini

ON DESTINY

Lined up on a station platform
grade school children
grade school children
grade school children
grade school children
talking, playing, eating.

"Aren't they cute."
"Remember?"
Lined up on a station platform
grown ups
grown ups
grown ups
grown ups
looking, talking, longing.

"Just fifty years and fifty billion kilometers."
"Remember?"
Lined up on a station platform
angels
angels
angels
angels
silent and watching
silent and glowing.

Shuntarō Tanikawa
Japan
Translated by Harold Wright

FOR GENEVIEVE *(Five Years Old)*

You clasp the little ball so tightly
One would have to break your hand
to wrest it,
As one breaks off the branch
To get the fruit . . .

And one waits . . .

A time comes
When the fruit just drops,
The time of ripeness.

And a time comes
When the world just falls,
The time of sleep.

Simeon Dumdum, Jr.
Philippines

CHILDHOOD IS THE ONLY LASTING FLOWER

1
Childhood is the only lasting flower.
When I go to bed each night
I still keep an eye open to watch the cuckoo's departure.

2
The movie theater is empty.
I only sense shadows of Indians
sharpening their arrows for Saturday matinee.

3
I would have been many things when I grew up.
Today in old chests I search for pieces of bygone time.
Childhood is the only lasting flower.

Ramón Díaz Eterovic
Chile
Translated by Teresa Rozo-Moorhouse

GOODNESS

I've always tried to be good
it's very demanding
I'm a real hound for
      doing something for someone
hold coats
    doors
      seats
get someone a job
   or something
open   up my arms
let someone have his cry on my shirt
but when I get my chance
I freeze completely
some kind of shyness maybe
I urge myself—do it
fling your arms wide
but it's difficult to sacrifice yourself
      when somebody's watching
so hard to be good
      for more than a few minutes
like holding your breath
however with daily practice
I have worked up to a whole hour
if nobody disturbs me
I sit all alone
with my watch in front of me
spreading my arms
    again and again
no trouble at all!
I am certainly best
when I'm all alone.

Benny Andersen
Denmark
Translated by Alexander Taylor

THE RHYTHM OF THE TOMTOM

The rhythm of the tomtom does not beat in my blood
Nor in my skin
Nor in my skin
The rhythm of the tomtom beats in my heart
In my heart
In my heart
The rhythm of the tomtom does not beat in my blood
Nor in my skin
Nor in my skin
The rhythm of the tomtom beats especially
In the way that I think
In the way that I think
I think Africa, I feel Africa, I proclaim Africa
I hate in Africa
I love in Africa
And I am Africa
The rhythm of the tomtom beats especially
In the way that I think
In the way that I think
I think Africa, I feel Africa, I proclaim Africa
And I become silent
Within you, for you, Africa
Within you, for you, Africa
A   fri   ca
        A   fri   ca
                A   fri   ca

António Jacinto
Angola
translated by Don Burness

Do what you like with my face.
If you find ruins
Or lies there—I won't be insulted.
Go where you want to—
To my old age or youth.
No, I won't look, I must hurry—
I must catch the next train.
Paint from your memory work in my hands
Or laziness, a caress or nothing.
And in the background—I beg you—
Paint a quiet life.

Amanda Aizpuriete
Latvia
Translated by Inguna Jansone

THE NEW SUIT

Striped suit,
a terrific tie,
buttoned shoes
and brown socks—
my outfit
for the party.

And the recommendations
drove me crazy—
—Don't eat ice cream
because it might drip.
—Juice, drink it slowly
since it dribbles.
—And nothing about
chocolate bombs
that might explode!
Happy birthday!
Who's that stuffed breathless
inside a tight suit?

Next year will be different.
I'll wear old clothes,
be ready to dribble,
and enjoy
ice cream, cake, and everything else.

Nidia Sanabria de Romero
Paraguay
Translated by Arnaldo D. Larrosa Morán with Naomi Shihab Nye

WHITE BRACELETS

we all have old scars
and sometimes in winter
I can still see what was
white bracelets
(let's call them white bracelets
just as my grandmother used to say
when we fell down steep stairways,
stop crying or you'll miss hearing
the stairs—they're still dancing)
what was once white bracelets
what before that showed pink
what before that was raw & festering
what before that was agony
down to the bones
what before that was
almost blacked out
& being dragged by the tractor
in the barbed wire
what before that was
surprise & yelling:
can't you STOP   STOP
what before that was
lying in the grass
reading a blue letter
looking up into sun & clouds
that were riffed
and quiet like white bracelets.

Colleen Thibaudeau
Canada

I HAVE TEN LEGS

When I run
I laugh with my legs.

When I run
I swallow the world with my legs.

When I run
I have ten legs.
All my legs
shout.

I exist
only when running.

Anna Swir
Poland
Translated by Czesław Miłosz and Leonard Nathan

THE TONGUE

You stick out your tongue
silver harpoon
hunting
between the glittering lips of darkness

Pia Tafdrup
Denmark
Translated by Monique M. Kennedy and Thomas E. Kennedy

A man comes in, his suit is crumpled
And thin-rimmed glasses are on his face.
He's arguing with the emptiness, he's crazy, he's a wind.
The thin-rimmed glasses quiver.
His suit is crumpled, he argues quickly.
The man comes in and fills the room.
The man comes in, he's been coming in for hours.
His suit is crumpled, he argues too quickly.
His glasses quiver, he's an idiot, he argues.
He's a wind, he's crazy, he's coming in.

Sergei Timofeyev
Latvia
Translated by Irina Osadchaya with Lyn Hejinian

GREENLAND'S HISTORY
—or the history of the Danes on Greenland

What were we doing up there
we Danish people
three thousand miles away
in the name of Hans Egede and Jakob Severin
what was the point of those crosses and all that expense?
What did we have in mind
when we collected the country's people in settlements
and then scattered them
and collected them in colonies
and then scattered them
and collected them in towns?
What was this magnificent plan we had conceived
with Christ and the Crown
we who crucify our Savior
and invest our king with a coin on his head?

For more than two hundred years they listened to us
like far too patient children
throughout a far too prolonged childhood.
When their wonderment came to an end
our own started
a grim wonderment
that an entire people should show so little gratitude.

Instead of visions we had come with principles
instead of feelings with our national church
and we excused ourselves
by saying it was no different at home.
As if the country's people
should make do with just as little
as we allow ourselves.

Then the country's people began to speak:
over the word Greenland they wrote their own name
Kalatdlit-Nunat
that means the people's land
over Egedesminde they wrote Ausiait
that means the Spiders
over Jakobshavn they wrote Ilulissat
that means the Ice Mountains
and thus it was they buried Hans Egede and Jakob Severin.
They no longer called themselves Greenlanders or Eskimos
but Inuit
that means people
and thus they began to reconquer
themselves with words.

Beneath the rock of silence
lies a multitude of names
and the right to these names
is owned by those who live in the language.

Sven Holm
Denmark
Translated by Paula Hostrup-Jessen

THE WALL

"A wall, don't you understand?
A wall before which I stand alone."
LUIS CERNUDA

the wall is high
very high
it has cracks where orderly ants live
they are not alone
the wall is several kilometers high
it almost touches the north star
the fleeting one
the double or the triple one
the star over the sea
—I was born under a good star they say
that is why now my star
has just struck this very high wall

Tania Diaz Castro
Cuba
Translated by Pablo Medina and
Carolina Hospital

JERUSALEM

On a roof in the Old City
laundry hanging in the late afternoon sunlight:
the white sheet of a woman who is my enemy,
the towel of a man who is my enemy,
to wipe off the sweat of his brow.

In the sky of the Old City
a kite.
At the other end of the string,
a child
I can't see
because of the wall.

We have put up many flags,
they have put up many flags.
To make us think that they're happy.
To make them think that we're happy.

Yehuda Amichai
Israel
Translated by Stephen Mitchell

There are times when I can't move.

I feel roots of mine everywhere,
as though all things were born of me,
or as though I were born of all things.

All I can do then is to stay still
with eyes open like two faces at the moment of birth,
with a small amount of love in one hand
and something cold in the other.

And all I can give someone passing by me
is that motionless absence
that has roots in him too.

Roberto Juarroz
Argentina
Translated by W. S. Merwin

In his room the man watches
light shine on the fruit

the apples gathering shadows
the shadows of resting pears

the watermelon's gash
of liquid pulp

the ancient figs
among solemn walnuts

at night in his room
the man watches fruit

Homero Aridjis
Mexico
Translated by Eliot Weinberger

THE INDIANS

The Indians
descend
maze after maze
with their emptiness on their backs.

In the past
they were warriors over all things.
They put up monuments to fire
and to the rains whose black fists
put the fruit in the earth.

In the theaters of their cities of colors
shone vestments
and crowns
and golden masks
brought from faraway enemy empires.

They marked time
with numerical precision.
They gave their conquerors
liquid gold to drink
and grasped the heavens
like a tiny flower.

In our day
they plow and seed the ground
the same as in primitive times.
Their women shape clay
and the stones of the field, or weave
while the wind
disorders their long, coarse hair,
    like that of goddesses.

I've seen them barefoot and almost nude,
in groups,
guarded by voices poised like whips,
or drunk and wavering with the pools of the setting sun
on the way back to their shacks
in the last block of the forgotten.

I've talked with them up in their refuges
there in the mountains watched over by idols
where they are happy as deer
but quiet and deep
as prisoners.

I've felt their faces
beat my eyes until the dying light
and so have discovered
my strength is neither
sound nor strong.

Next to their feet
that all the roads destroyed
I leave my own blood
written on an obscure bough.

Roberto Sosa
Honduras
Translated by Jim Lindsey

THE LABOURER

The labourer is back from the field
when sunset dies away from the sky
opening the way to darkness.

The labourer is back from the field
with his huge tiredness
hanging on his shoulders.

Night finds him sleeping
under a blanket of boredom.

Life starting at dawn,
ending at dusk.

He prays for courage.
May his bit of food
not slip from his plate.

Toolsy Daby
Mauritius

CLOUDS ON THE SEA

I walk among men with tall bones,
With shoes of leather, and pink faces;
I meet no man holding a begging bowl;
All have their dwelling places.

In my country
Every child is taught to read and write,
Every child has shoes and a warm coat,
Every child must eat his dinner,
No one must grow any thinner;
It is considered remarkable and not nice
To meet bed-bugs or lice.
Oh we live like the rich
With music at the touch of a switch,
Light in the middle of the night,
Water in the house as from a spring,
Hot, if you wish, or cold, anything
For the comfort of the flesh,
In my country. Fragment
Of new skin at the edge of the world's ulcer.

For the question
That troubled you as you watched the reapers
And a poor woman following,
Gleaning ears on the ground,
Why should I have grain and this woman none?
No satisfactory answer has ever been found.

Ruth Dallas
New Zealand

OR

He went out of the room in which he was praying. He spent there
years and years.

He seemed as if he just came out of the depth of an ocean,
or out of the heart of a pearl,
or out of a whale,
or out of the core of an emerald,
or out of the center of the sun,
or out of a gold vein,
or out of a drop of dew,
or out of a cloud,
or out of the eye of a star,
or out of the light of the eye,
or out of the pulse of a heart,
or out of the secret of the secret,
or out of the secret of the word,
or out of the heart of glory,
or out of the cradle of creation,
or out of the generosity of love,
or out of the core of mercy,
or out of the arms of a mother,
or out of the depth of whisper,
or out of the silence of fear,
or out of the tenderness of forgiveness,
or out of the river of purgatory,
or out of the chandelier of ethics,
or out of the warmth of sincerity,
or out of the fervor of passion,
or out of the beauty of perfection,
or out of the perfection of beauty,
or out of the core of obedience,
or out of the harmony of the universe,
or out of the beauty of sublimity,
or out of the core of beauty,

or out of the transparency of clairvoyance,
or out of the smoothness of light,
or out of the heart of serenity,
or out of the flower's honey,
or out of the joy of thanks,
or out of the spontaneity of purity,
or out of the simplicity of simple nature,
or out of the ancient beach.

    He stood and looked around him, and what he saw made him return to his room and close the door behind him.

Ali Darwish
Egypt
Translated by the poet

MY SHARE

everyone's busy with something
that granny spinning wool
with hands like dried, shrunken cucumbers
left in the field
after the seeds were taken out,
she is busy with something;
the wheeler-dealer who buys and sells land
and the student who is examined
on what he wasn't taught
are busy with something;
the cashier who wonders about the connection
between his hands and the money he counts endlessly
and the manager who married off his elder daughter yesterday,
the pilot getting ready for a new flight
with his bag that has seen so many countries,
the fireman who has spent a day without trouble
and his memories of fires,
the worker who wakes up for the night shift
and his sleeping anger,
that chicken in the litter is busy with something
getting ready for chicks like cotton-candy,

and what is left for me to do is write poetry.

Salih Bolat
Turkey
Translated by Yusuf Eradam

PRIDE

I tell you, even rocks crack,
and not because of age.
For years they lie on their backs
in the heat and the cold,
so many years,
it almost seems peaceful.
They don't move, so the cracks stay hidden.
A kind of pride.
Years pass over them, waiting there.
Whoever is going to shatter them
hasn't come yet.
And so the moss flourishes, the seaweed
whips around,
the sea pushes through and rolls back—
the rocks seem motionless.
Till a little seal comes to rub against them,
comes and goes away.
And suddenly the rock has an open wound.
I told you, when rocks break, it happens by surprise.
And people, too.

Dahlia Ravikovitch
Israel
Translated by Chana Bloch and Ariel Bloch

LUCIA

I was born woman.
They say my eyes were very bright
and they called me Lucia,
the one who gives light.

> The fishermen leave early in the morning,
> on fragile boats.
> The women wave their hands from the pier.
> They don't know when the men will return.

> Every night, when the moon and the stars
> are the only lights,
> all the women of town gather on the pier again
> and sing to the asters,
> invoke them to guide their men home.

My father was proud of me.
Two hours after the birth
he threw a bottle of anisette
on the door of the house
to wash the newborn with sweetness
and good luck.

> She was a princess,
> her eyes the most beautiful of the island,
> the kingdom of her father the richest.

> When the armed men
> broke into the walls of the city
> she was found brushing her hair
> by the window on the water.

> He loved her at once.
> and offered her the life of her father
> and the kingdom.
> She refused.
> He took her eyes, her hair,
> burned down the city and left the island again.

Bats are blind.
They travel through the night
without candles.
I was born woman,
they call me Lucia,
but the journey is a long one
and the lighthouse still far.

Lucia Casalinuovo
Italy

FAR AND CLOSE

You
Look a while at me,
Look a while at a cloud.

I feel
You are far away while looking at me,
So very close while looking at the cloud.

Gu Cheng
China
Translated by Edward Morin

AT THE FERRY

They shall all be here one day.
You are in the western hemisphere
And you are in the far South.
Who are you waiting alone and wearied
In the wintry North?
I am the East, we shall all be meeting at the ferry.

Now there's only a vast expanse of sand—
Dark waters in the distance, the deserted jetty
And snakeskins lying upside down.
The moaning wind roams about pining for human touch
Turns round and goes back again and again.

And yet this will come about, this meeting, one day.
They will collect in a big crowd
Or in small groups of twos and threes,
Sure of themselves and silently
On a moonless night or under a full moon in total eclipse.
The mysterious ferry stays awake, waiting.

Vijaya Mukhopadhyay
India
Translated by the poet

NOTES ON THE CONTRIBUTORS

The poets whose works appear in this book are from sixty-eight countries around the world.

AMANDA AIZPURIETE (Latvia, b. 1956) has translated Emily Dickinson into Latvian and is now busy bringing up four children.

SUNAY AKIN (Turkey, b. 1962) has published two books of poetry and lives in Istanbul.

YEHUDA AMICHAI (Israel, b. 1924 in Germany) often writes of his "childhood of blessed memory" and says he was formed "half by the ethics of [his] father and half by the cruelties of war."

BENNY ANDERSEN (Denmark, b. 1929) was a musician before becoming well known for his children's books, radio and television comedies, and collections of short stories and poems.

HOMERO ARIDJIS (Mexico, b. 1940) lives in Mexico City. His new novel is set in 1492 and is entitled *The Life of Cabezon.*

NASIMA AZIZ (India) has published a book of poems through the Writers Workshop of Calcutta. When Naomi Shihab Nye was speaking to a group of writers at a library in India she discussed *This Same Sky* and was given a piece of paper with the handwritten poem "Home" on it by a man who later disappeared into the crowd.

SALEEM BARAKAT (Syria, b. 1951) is of Kurdish origin. He has worked as a journalist and editor, and presently lives in Cyprus.

MIRON BIALOSZEWSKI (Poland, 1922–1983) once started a little theater in which his ten fingers were the actors. He wrote odes to colanders, quilts, keys, and dusty floors.

ALBERTO BLANCO (Mexico, b. 1951) has published children's books as well as poetry, and has been a keyboard player and singer for jazz-rock groups.

SALIH BOLAT (Turkey, b. 1956) has published three books of poems and lives in Ankara.

POUL BORUM (Denmark, b. 1934) is an art and literary critic. He has written films and libretti for opera, and edits the only magazine of children's poetry in Denmark.

EKA BUDIANTA (Indonesia, b. 1956) studied Japanese literature, and has worked for the BBC in London. One of his books is entitled *Bang Bang Toot!*

JORGE CARRERA ANDRADE (Ecuador, b. 1903) edited a magazine when he was still a teenager and later was Ecuadorian consul to China, Japan, and the United States/San Francisco.

LUCIA CASALINUOVO (Italy, b. 1954) grew up in Petrizzi, which means "made of rocks," a town abandoned since its last, worst earthquake. She writes: "I played house among the rosemary bushes of the town's cemetery, ate tons of prickled pears, and caught baby frogs while my mother did the laundry by the river. Every Sunday morning I rode in a basket on my mother's back down the trail to the beach, where I lost my piece of parmigiano cheese in the sand more than once. . . ."

NIRENDRANATH CHAKRAVARTI (India, b. 1924) has been a journalist and editor of a teen magazine, author of more than 20 books of poems, and is presently working on the spelling norms of Bengali words.

CHANG SHIANG-HUA (Taiwan, b. 1939) grew up loving the simple tranquility of the countryside and has been writing poems since age nineteen. She has taught high school and college, and has represented China at international conferences of writers.

KIM CHIHA (South Korea, b. 1941), a leading activist against governmental corruption since his youth, was imprisoned and tortured many times. He has finally been recognized as a national hero and allowed to return to his family.

JOSÉ CRAVEIRINHA (Mozambique, b. 1922) has worked as a journalist and is now a librarian.

TOOLSY DABY (Mauritius, b. 1938) writes in English and French, and has been a journalist, teacher, novelist, playwright, and comedian.

RUTH DALLAS (New Zealand, b. 1919) has written children's books, adult novels, and poems.

ALI DARWISH (Egypt, b. 1944) is the author of four collections of stories, a professional translator, author of numerous articles about Sufism, and an expert on Cairo's spectacular Khan el-Khalili Bazaar.

MAHMUD DARWISH (Palestine, b. 1941) has lived in exile in Cairo and Paris and wrote his first poem at age eight. It was about his village being lost to occupation: "My father's silence still rings more loudly in my ears than any bell."

JIBANANDA DAS (India) was a professor of English but wrote poems entirely in Bengali.

MANJUSH DASGUPTA (India, b. 1942), an economist by profession, has edited three anthologies of contemporary poetry and has translated modern French poems.

ALEŠ DEBELJAK (Slovenia, b. 1960) teaches comparative religion in Ljubljana and is the author of numerous books including *Anxious Moments* and *A Dictionary of Silence*.

TANIA DIAZ CASTRO (Cuba, b. 1939) has worked as a journalist and an advocate for human rights in her country. She is presently under house arrest in Havana.

RAMÓN DÍAZ ETEROVIC (Chile, b. 1956) edits a poetry magazine called *The Pure Drop*, is a member of the Society of Writers of Chile, and is the author of many books of poems and stories, including *The Absent Passenger* and *The City is Sad*.

WIMAL DISSANAYAKE (Sri Lanka, b. 1939) has published books in the United States dealing with literature and film as well as poetry books written in his native Sinhalese.

ZUHUR DIXON (Iraq, b. 1933) has lived in Baghdad for many years and has published several collections of poetry, including *A Homeland for Everything*.

CARLOS DRUMMOND DE ANDRADE (Brazil, b. 1902) grew up in a small mining town where his father was a rancher, was expelled from a Jesuit school for "mental insubordination," has spent his grown life in Rio de Janeiro, and has long been one of Brazil's best-loved writers.

SIMEON DUMDUM, JR. (Philippines) studied for the priesthood in Ireland but left the seminary to become a lawyer.

GEVORG EMIN (Armenia, b. 1919) says his own poetry springs from the town of Ashtarag, where he grew up, "and the deep valley of the Kassakh River, where since my earliest childhood I heard the running water." The poet has written more than thirty books of poetry and prose in his native Armenia, "a very small nation with a very old history, and a very large heart."

YUSUF ERADAM (Turkey, b. 1954) is associate professor at Ankara University in the Department of American Culture and Literature. He writes poetry and stories and translates for the only translation magazine in his country. He says "poetry translation is my favorite." If "A Brief Note to the Bag Lady, Ma Sister" is read aloud, the poet suggests Enya's "Lothlórien," from her latest album, *Shepherd Moons*, as suitable background music.

DAVID ESCOBAR GALINDO (El Salvador, b. 1943) is a writer, poet, and lawyer. He dedicated his book, *Poems to Paint a Small Country*, from which "A Short Story" is taken, to his niece Evelyn-Pirulina, who lives in Madison, Wisconsin. Like so many other Salvadoran children today, Evelyn is growing up far away from her homeland. According to the poet, even if these children don't know it yet, "El Salvador is in their blood; it is their history, it is a fundamental part of their fabric that they will need to understand as they grow." In 1990 the government appointed him to the dialogue commission for negotiating peace and ending the country's eleven-year-old civil war.

LIBER FALCO (Uruguay, 1906–1955) wrote lyrics exploring the themes of death, solitude, and time. Teresa Anderson, translator of his poem included here, first heard these words as a song performed by Daniel Vigletti, a Uruguayan folk musician.

MUHAMMAD AL-FAYIZ (Kuwait, b. 1938) has worked in radio and television for the Ministry of Information and often expresses a nostalgia for the pre-oil past in his poems.

RENÉE FERRER DE ARRÉLLAGA (Paraguay) is a poet, novelist, and editor of children's poetry.

MUHAMMAD AL-GHUZZI (Tunisia, b. 1949) was born in the ancient city of Qairwan and has worked as a teacher. He has also translated Swedish poetry into Arabic.

GU GHENG (China, b. 1956) is the son of poet Gu Gong and the youngest of the Misty Poets group. He helped found the nonofficial literary journal *Today* in 1974 and lives in exile with his wife in New Zealand and Germany.

ALAMGIR HASHMI (Pakistan) a University Professor of English and Comparative Literature at Islamabad, is an anglophone poet and has published ten collections of his poetry and several volumes of literary criticism, and has also translated works from the Urdu and Punjabi languages. In 1989 he recorded a reading of his poems for the archives of the Library of Congress.

JAVIER HERAUD (Peru, 1942–1963) published two books of poems and died by assassination.

LETICIA HERRERA ALVAREZ (Mexico, b. 1954) has written for newspapers, television, and the cinema in Mexico and Costa Rica.

FLORIA HERRERO PINTO (Costa Rica, b. 1943) has published several books of literature for children in Costa Rica and Venezuela.

NAZIM HIKMET (Turkey, 1902–1963) spent much of his lifetime traveling, in exile, and in prison on various political charges. Artists from many countries campaigned for his freedom. He circulated poems in letters to his family.

SVEN HOLM (Denmark, b. 1940) is a novelist, short-story writer, poet, and dramatist. He wrote the poem included in this volume after visiting Greenland in 1977.

MIROSLAV HOLUB (Czechoslovakia, b. 1923) is an eminent scientist involved in immunology research as well as a writer. He says of both his professions, "I was most lucky in my life to do, in spite of all adversities, exactly what I liked."

KYONGJOO HONG RYOU (South Korea, b. 1959) grew up on a small farm, on a mountain overlooking a small river which ran across the rice fields. "Our mountain maintained its stunning beauty all seasons, in spring with azaleas, in summer with acacias and wild flowers, in autumn with coloring leaves and in winter, snow on evergreens. I started to write poetry in fourth grade and ever since then poetry has been my mother tongue."

VICENTE HUIDOBRO (Chile, 1893–1948) lived in Paris for many years and wrote in both Spanish and French.

ZIA HYDER (Bangladesh, b. 1936) studied theater in Hawaii, San Francisco, and New York, and is presently a professor of dramatic arts, as well as a poet, playwright, and essayist.

IKU TAKENAKA (Japan, b. 1904) founded a noted poetry magazine for children called *Giraffe*.

ANTÓNIO JACINTO (Angola, b. 1924) has long struggled for his country's independence. Presently retired, he received the important NOMA prize for publishing in Africa in 1986.

ROLF JACOBSEN (Norway, b. 1907) launched poetic modernism in Norway with his first book, *Earth and Iron*, published in 1933.

TOMASZ JASTRUN (Poland, b. 1950) claims he is the best tennis player of all Polish poets and the best poet of all Polish tennis players.

JEAN JOUBERT (France, b. 1928) has published novels and children's stories as well as poetry, and teaches American literature in Montpellier.

ROBERTO JUARROZ (Argentina, b. 1925) has worked as a librarian and has published nine volumes of poems.

NICOLAI KANTCHEV (Bulgaria) wrote a book of poems called *Medusa*, from which the poem in this collection is taken.

JAAN KAPLINSKI (Estonia, b. 1941) is one of eastern Europe's most widely known poets, as well as a translator, essayist, professor, and serious student of Mahayana Buddhism.

TYMOTEUSZ KARPOWICZ (Poland, b. 1921) has worked as a journalist and is known as a poet "in love with Earth." (Czesław Miłosz)

PRAMILA KHADUN (Mauritius, b. 1950) teaches home economics in a secondary school and has been writing poems for eighteen years.

FAWZIYYA ABU KHALID (Saudi Arabia, b. 1955) published her first volume of poems at the age of eighteen and teaches at the Girls' University College of King Saud University.

KWANG-KYU KIM (South Korea, b. 1941) is a professor of German language and literature and has won major Korean literary prizes for his own poetry.

KLARA KOETTNER-BENIGNI (Austria, b. 1928) has published poetry and novels and has written essays on East European poetry.

KANDEMIR KONDUK (Turkey, b. 1945) is a writer of drama and comedy. His plays have been produced by many theater groups, and he has written television comedy for the last twenty years.

CHRISTINE M. KRISHNASAMI (India) has experimented in a variety of poetic forms, publishing books covered in beautiful sari cloth through the Writers Workshop of Calcutta.

TOM KRISTENSEN (Denmark, 1893–1974) introduced the works of numerous writers, including Ernest Hemingway and James Joyce, into Scandinavia and translated them. He also wrote a well-known novel entitled *Havoc*.

KARL KROLOW (Germany, b. 1915) has published over thirty-five volumes of his poems, essays, and translations.

LAN NGUYEN (Vietnam, b. 1960) was raised in a small mountain town called Da-lat, which she describes as "the most beautiful place in the world." She lost two brothers in the war. Now she is an engineer with "a good husband and two beautiful children."

INGEMAR LECKIUS (Sweden, b. 1928) published his first book *Other Rites* in 1951 and is also a critic and translator. He says "Locked In" expresses "the universe of solitude . . . common to all youth."

MUHAMMAD AL-MAGHUT (Syria, b. 1934) is self-educated and has written plays that are performed throughout the Arab world.

JAYANTA MAHAPATRA (India, b. 1928) has traveled widely throughout the world to read his poems and has also been a lecturer in physics.

AL MAHMUD (Bangladesh) has been called "one of the most refreshingly original poets of contemporary Bangladesh."

ALI AL-MAK (the Sudan, b. 1937) is a professor at the University of Khartoum and President of the Sudanese Writers' Union. He published his first story at the age of sixteen and has recently published in *Short Story International*. He often writes about the moods and attitudes of the people of his hometown, Omdurman.

FARHAD MAZHAR (Bangladesh, b. 1946) often draws on scientific ideas and vocabulary for his poetry.

CECILIA MEIRELES (Brazil, 1901–1964) was born in Rio de Janeiro and raised by her grandmother after the early death of her parents. She always viewed her poems as being independent of any literary movement. One of her books, *Poems Written in India*, expressed her deep interest in Indian culture and mysticism. She also translated Indian poets into Portuguese and wrote books for children. Some of her favorite recurrent images were birds, wind, sky, and sea.

MÁIRE MHAC AN TSAOI (Ireland, b. 1922) has worked hard for the preservation of the Irish language.

GUADALUPE MORFÍN (Mexico, b. 1953) has studied law, theology, and social sciences, and works for the publishing department of the University of Guadalajara. One of her books is called *The Hope of the Angel*.

VIJAYA MUKHOPADHYAY (India, b. 1937) has been active in the modern Bengali poetry movement since 1964, publishing books, editing journals, participating in international seminars and lectures, and working with translations.

LES MURRAY (Australia, b. 1938) says, "I am interested in one thing only and that is grace. I found this instrument called poetry and. . . . I do it over and over again to bring to myself and others the experience of grace." One of the most acclaimed and widely traveled poets of Australia, Murray also says he has been "happy to learn a lot from the Aborigines."

MUSŌ SOSEKI (Japan) was a thirteenth-century Zen teacher with students numbering more than 13,000, as well as the father of the Japanese rock garden.

PABLO NERUDA (Chile, 1904–1973), one of the great world poets of the twentieth century, worked for many years as a diplomat, received the Nobel Prize for Literature, and was often referred to as "the poet of enslaved humanity."

STELLA NGATHO (Kenya, b. 1953) writes "out of the song and ritual of an older tribal reality" (Deirdre Lashgari).

MUNEER NIAZI (Pakistan) is a poet whose work was translated by the late beloved poet/professor of Peshawar, Daud Kanal.

LESLIE NORRIS (Wales, b. 1921) has taught in Wales and Utah, is a passionate lover of animals, and has made tapes of his poems for children.

A.Z.M. OBAIDULLAH KHAN (Bangladesh) is the author of *Prayer for Rain and the Brave of Heart* and has been Minister of Agriculture for his country.

TOMMY OLOFSSON (Sweden, b. 1950) earns his living as a poet and literary critic. He lives in the countryside outside the ancient university town of Lund with his wife, four daughters, and two cats. His book *Elemental Poems* has recently been published in the U.S. by White Pine Press.

MICHAEL ONDAATJE (Canada, b. 1943) was born in Sri Lanka, lives in Toronto, writes, and dances. His book *The Cinnamon Peeler* contains poems spanning twenty-five years.

KEMAL OZER (Turkey, b. 1935) lives in Istanbul and is one of the most prolific and active figures of the contemporary Turkish literary scene.

BIBHU PADHI (India, b. 1951) writes prolifically in English and has published widely. Many recent poems explore his relationship with his young sons.

GIEVE PATEL (India, b. 1940) is a poet, painter, playwright, and general medical practitioner with a clinic in central Bombay.

OCTAVIO PAZ (Mexico, b. 1914), one of the best-known poets of Latin America, has also served as a diplomat in Asia and Europe.

TONY PEREZ (Philippines) is a playwright, fiber artist, book designer, puppeteer, and creator of original patterns for hand knitting.

KEVIN PERRYMAN (Bavaria, b. 1950 in England) has lived in Germany for the last twenty years and edits *Babel*, a poetry and translation magazine.

ALINE PETTERSSON (Mexico, b. 1938) writes poetry, short stories, and children's stories, and has been invited to many countries to share her work.

VASKO POPA (Yugoslavia, 1922–1991) wrote poems that have been translated into almost every European language. His books include *Crust, Field of Sleeplessness,* and *Secondary Heaven.*

BUNDGÅRD POVLSEN (Denmark, b. 1918) was first trained as a blacksmith and later became a journalist.

ALFONSO QUIJADA URÍAS (El Salvador) has published *They Come and Knock on the Door* through Curbstone Press in Connecticut.

DAHLIA RAVIKOVITCH (Israel, b. 1936) was raised on a collective farm and studied English literature at the Hebrew University in Jerusalem.

TARAPADA RAY (India, b. 1936) has worked in government services and has been the editor or author of nearly thirty books, including books of poems, children's stories, and best-selling light features.

FUAD RIFKA (Lebanon, b. 1930) has a Ph.D. in philosophy and has taught at various universities in Beirut.

YANNIS RITSOS (Greece, b. 1909) is the celebrated author of more than 115 books of poetry, translations, essays, and dramatic works. He began painting, playing the piano, and writing poetry at the age of eight.

BLANCA RODRIGUEZ (Mexico, b. 1944) works as a literary counselor at the National Fine Arts Institute in Mexico City.

TADEUSZ RÓŻEWICZ (Poland, b. 1921) first published poems related to his traumatic war experiences and has also written plays.

YUSUF AL-SA'IGH (Iraq, b. 1933) is a poet, short-story writer, and critic, with a deep interest in painting.

SHIHAB SARKAR (Bangladesh, b. 1952) had many playmates as a child but often preferred reading in seclusion, especially fairy tales, ghost stories, and thrillers. He was fond of storms, small animals, and birds, and disliked quarrels, dust, grammar, and heat.

NIDIA SANABRIA DE ROMERO (Paraguay, b. 1928) has long been involved in children's theater, and is the founder and principal of the Iberoamericano High School.

BENILDA S. SANTOS (Philippines) writes poems in both Filipino and English and is also an assistant professor of Filipino literature.

TIALUGA SUNIA SELOTI (American Samoa, b. 1954) became known early as a storyteller among her friends, is a deaconess at her Congregational church, and has studied in New Zealand and Hawaii.

SAMARENDRA SENGUPTA (India) edits a leading literary journal of Bengal, and has published eight books of poems.

SAMEENEH SHIRAZIE (Pakistan) lives in Karachi and has a master's degree in English Literature. She is the mother of a new baby daughter named Noor, Arabic for "light."

SHUNTARŌ TANIKAWA (Japan, b. 1931) wrote a five-volume translation of *Mother Goose* and has translated the comic strip "Peanuts" since 1969. His translator Harold Wright writes, "He entered a poetry contest because he didn't want to study for his college entrance exams and went on to become one of Japan's best-known contemporary poets. . . . Like a businessman, he goes each morning to his studio–office to spend most of his day writing. To write something every day is an obsession with him, he admits. He still composes song lyrics, is a major advocate of poetry readings . . . and has been known to shout his poetry via bullhorn from the windows of office buildings."

JON SILKIN (England, b. 1930) has been called one of the true "independents" of contemporary British poetry.

R. A. SIMPSON (Australia, b. 1929) has written criticism for various magazines and was a lecturer in art.

EDITH SÖDERGRAN (Finland, 1892–1923) was born of Swedish parents and wrote in Swedish, though she also spoke Russian and German fluently. She published her work while very young and died of tuberculosis at age thirty-one.

ROBERTO SOSA (Honduras, b. 1930) has written poetry that, at various times, has been both banned and highly honored in his own country, since he explores deeply the subjects of oppression and poverty.

SHARON STEVENSON (Canada) was born in Ontario and lived in Vancouver.

RAMÓN C. SUNICO (Philippines, b. 1955) publishes children's books and poetry, wears his hair long, and collects earrings.

LINUS SURYADI AG (Indonesia) was the second son of ten children born to a Javanese farming family, and has read and published his poems widely.

ANNA SWIR (Poland, 1909–1984) published her first book of poetry at age twenty-five and continued publishing very original and energetic poems past the age of sixty.

PIA TAFDRUP (Denmark, b. 1952) is one of her country's leading poets, and edited *Transformationer*, an anthology of Danish poetry of the 1980s.

TATSUJI MIYOSHI (Japan, 1900–1964) had a degree in French literature and helped to establish a new lyricism in Japanese poetry.

COLLEEN THIBAUDEAU (Canada, b. 1925) says, "When you're a grandmother, you've done just about everything."

SERGEI TIMOFEYEV (Latvia, b. 1970) dreams about writing a small book that he could tuck secretly into the pockets of his friends.

PETER VAN TOORN (Canada, b. 1944 in Holland) has played tenor sax in a blues band and works as an English teacher in Montreal.

TOMAS TRANSTRÖMER (Sweden, b. 1931) has long been one of the leading poets of his country as well as an occupational psychologist and pianist.

NADIA TUENI (Lebanon) died in 1983. Her book *Lebanon: Twenty Poems for One Love* was a "poetic geography" for the Lebanon she knew prior to its tragic ravaging. She was married to the ambassador of Lebanon to the United Nations.

FADWA TUQAN (Palestine, b. 1917) has been publishing poetry since 1952, and finds the notion of fleeing her own land to live in another country "unthinkable."

ANDREI VOZNESENSKY (Russia, b. 1933) first dreamed of being a painter, studied architecture, and became a poet after a fire destroyed an elaborate architectural project he had worked on for a year. His books and readings, even on prime-time television in his country, have made him as well known as a film star among his people, and he has traveled and published widely abroad.

XU DE-MIN (China, b. 1953) teaches at Fudan University in Shanghai.

XUE DI (China, b. 1957) lived as a child in the beautiful region of Hangzhou, surrounded by "lakes, tourists, and constant mist from the rain, and many little mountains." Later he suffered "the brutality of the Communist Party" during the Cultural Revolution and in 1990 came to the United States.

RICARDO YÁÑEZ (Mexico, b. 1948) is the director of creative writing at the University of Guadalajara. He has coordinated literary workshops in various states of Mexico.

ZOLTÁN ZELK (Hungary, b. 1906) lived for many years in his own country under an assumed name and spent terms in prison for political activities.

THIS

Finland
Sweden
Norway   Estonia
Denmark   Poland Latvia
Germany
Bavaria   Austria
Czechoslovakia   Hungary
60   Yugoslavia
Ireland   Slovenia Turkey
Wales   Bulgaria Armenia
England   France   Syria
          Italy   Russia
          Greece   Iraq   South Korea
30 N Tunisia   Kuwait   China   Japan
      Egypt   Pakistan   Taiwan
Lebanon   Saudi   India   Philippines
Palestine Israel Arabia   Bangladesh
Mali   The Sudan   Vietnam
                              Sri Lanka
0   Cameroon Kenya   Indonesia

Angola
Mozambique   Mauritius   Australia
30 S

60

Every poet included in THIS SAME SKY *is represented here by a star.* ✳

SAME SKY

Greenland

Canada

60

N 30

Cuba

Mexico

Honduras

El Salvador

Costa Rica

Ecuador

0

Peru

Brazil

Paraguay

American Samoa

S 30

Uruguay

New Zealand

Chile

Argentina

60

Map by Virginia Norey

SUGGESTIONS FOR FURTHER READING

These excellent anthologies bring together poems written by poets who live in the United States or who called the United States home. The asterisks indicate volumes published especially for younger readers.

The Best American Poetry 1991, edited by Mark Strand. David Lehman, series editor. New York: Collier Books, 1991.

A Book of Women Poets from Antiquity to Now, edited by Aliki Barnstone and Willis Barnstone. New York: Schocken Books, 1980, 1992. This volume collects poets from many countries including the United States.

* *Favorite Poems Old and New,* selected by Helen Ferris. New York: Doubleday, 1957.

The Forgotten Language, edited by Christopher Merrill. Salt Lake City: Peregrine Smith Books, 1991.

* *Going Over to Your Place: Poems for Each Other,* selected by Paul B. Janeczko. New York: Bradbury Press, 1987.

The Morrow Anthology of Younger American Poets, edited by Dave Smith and David Bottoms. New York: Quill, 1985.

New American Poets of the 90's, edited by Jack Myers and Roger Weingarten. Boston: David R. Godine, 1991.

* *The Place My Words Are Looking For,* selected by Paul B. Janeczko. New York: Bradbury Press, 1990.

* *Strings: A Gathering of Family Poems,* selected by Paul B. Janeczko. New York: Bradbury Press, 1984.

* *Talking to the Sun: An Illustrated Anthology of Poems for Young People,* selected by Kenneth Koch and Kate Farrell. New York: The Metropolitan Museum of Art/ Henry Holt, 1985. This volume collects poets from many countries including the United States.

* *This Delicious Day, 65 Poems,* selected by Paul B. Janeczko, New York: Orchard Books, 1987.

Under 35: The New Generation of American Poets, edited by Nicholas Christopher. New York: Anchor/Doubleday, 1989.

ACKNOWLEDGMENTS

The scope of this volume made it occasionally difficult—despite sincere and sustained effort—to locate poets and/or their executors. The compiler and editor in chief regret any omissions or errors. If you wish to contact the publisher, corrections will be made in subsequent printings.

Permission to reprint copyrighted material is gratefully acknowledged to the following:

Amanda Aizpuriete, ☀ for "Do what you like with my face," copyright © 1988 by Amanda Aizpuriete. **Daisy Aldan,** ☽ for "Dawn" by Edith Södergran, translated by Daisy Aldan, copyright © 1992 by Daisy Aldan, and "Cat" by Jibananda Das, translated by Lila Ray from *Poems from India*, edited by Daisy Aldan, copyright © by Daisy Aldan with Leif Sjöberg. **Sunay Akin,** ✷ for "Debt," translated by Yusuf Eradam, copyright © by Sunay Akin. **Teresa Anderson,** ☀ for "I was born in Jacinto Vera," by Liber Falco, translated by Teresa Anderson, copyright © 1992 by Teresa Anderson. **Nasima Aziz,** ☽ for "Home," copyright © by Nasima Aziz and the Writers Workshop of Calcutta. **Bantam Doubleday Dell Publishing Group,** ✷ for "Love" by Tymoteusz Karpowicz, and "Transformations" by Tadeusz Różewicz from *Postwar Polish Poetry*, edited by Czesław Miłosz, copyright © 1965 by Czesław Miłosz. **Ben Bennani,** ☀ for "The Prison Cell" by Mahmud Darwish, translated by Ben Bennani, copyright © Ben Bennani. **Constance E. Berkley,** ☽ for "The Gatherer" from *The City of Dust* by Ali al-Mak, translated and edited by al-Fatih Mahjoub and Constance E. Berkley, published by Sudanese Publication Series (No. II), Embassy of the Democratic Republic of The Sudan, copyright © 1982 by Constance E. Berkley. **Alberto Blanco,** ✷ for "Horse by Moonlight," translated by Jennifer Clement, and "The Parakeets," translated by W. S. Merwin, copyright © by Alberto Blanco. **Chana Bloch,** ☀ for "Wildpeace" by Yehuda Amichai from *Tikkua* (vol. 2, no. 2), translated by Chana Bloch, copyright © 1987 by Chana Bloch, and "Magic" and "Pride" by Dahlia Ravikovitch from *The Window*, translated and edited by Chana and Ariel Bloch, copyright © 1989 by Chana Bloch. **Salih Bolat,** ☽ for "My Share," translated by Yusuf Eradam, copyright © 1992 by Salih Bolat. **Daniel Bourne,** ✷ for "Father and Son" by Tomasz Jastrun, translated by Daniel Bourne, copyright © by Daniel Bourne. **John Malcolm Brinnin,** ☀ for "Life of a Cricket" by Jorge Carrera Andrade, translated by John Malcolm Brinnin, from *Contemporary World Poets*, edited by Donald Junkins, published by Harcourt Brace Jovanovich, copyright © 1976 by John Malcolm Brinnin. **Don Burness,** ☽ for "A Man Never Cries" by José Craveirinha, and "The Rhythm of the Tomtom" by António Jacinto, translated by Don Burness, from *A Horse of White Clouds—Poems for Lusophone Africa*, published by Ohio University Press, copyright © by Don Burness. **Lucia Casalinuovo,** ✷ for "Lucia" (first appeared in *Pax*, vol. IV, no. 1), copyright © 1987 by Lucia Casalinuovo. **Nirendranath Chakravarti,** ☀ for "The Garden of a Child," copyright © 1992 by Nirendranath Chakravarti. **Chang Shiang-hua,** ☽ for "Wordless Day" and "An Appointment," copyright © by Chang Shiang-hua. **The Charioteer Press,** ✷ for " 'Oh! Oh! Should They Take Away My Stove . . .' My Inexhaustible Ode to Joy" by Miron Bialoszewski, translated by Bogdan Czaykowski and Andrzej Busza, from *The Revolution of Things*, copyright © 1974 by Bogdan Czaykowski and Andrzej Busza. **Columbia University Press & Salma Khadra Jayyusi,** ☀ for "The Pen" by Muhammad al-Ghuzzi, "The Orphan" by Muhammad al-Maghut, "The Squirrel" by Saleem Barakat, "Ants" by Yusuf al-Sa'igh, and "The Overture" by Zuhur Dixon, from *Modern Arabic Poetry, an Anthology*, edited by Salma Khadra Jayyusi, copyright © 1987 by Columbia University Press, New York. **Copper Canyon Press,** ☽ for "In the Kitchen" and "Childhood" from *Black Iris* by Jean Joubert, translated by Denise Levertov, copyright © 1988 by Denise Levertov. **Curbstone Press,** ✷ for "There's an Orange Tree Out There," from *They*

INDEX TO COUNTRIES

INDEX TO POETS

EFFORTS OF MAURITIUS IN THE FIGHT FOR FREEDOM 1939-45
Rs 10
MAURITIUS
MAURITIUS
3.00
中華民國郵票
REPUBLIC OF CHINA
1.40
Air Mail
7 15PM
5 NOV
1991
Postcode
39p
Naomi Shihab Nye
48
Canada

GUYANA
$6.40
SIAM
THAILAND
FLYGPOST · PAR AVION
Guyana SOUTH AMERICA
80
POSTAGE AND REVENUE
NIPPON
41
62
S. SHIRAZEE
5.00
भारत INDIA
ogramme